Cocobolo

also by C. G. Wayne

WTexas in 2 Plays

French Defense

Cocobolo

Reprise 2011

By C. G. Wayne

Otter Track Press

MRose Group, LLC
Wetumpka, Al

Otter Track Press

Otter Track Press is an imprint of MRose Group, LLC. Wetumpka, Alabama. (www.mrose.com)

The hardcover edition of this book was published in 2013 by Otter Track Press

FIRST TRADE PAPERBACK EDITION PUBLISHED 2014.

Wayne, Clifford Gordon.
Cocobolo, reprise 2011 / by C.G. Wayne—1st ed.

Summary: A collection of short stories that form a story cycle of seven Gulf Coast expatriates and residents.

Library of Congress Control Number: 2013915789
ISBN 978-0-9848229-3-5
[1. Fiction—Literature. 2. Post-modern—Fiction. 3. Cocobolo—Story Cycle]

Acknowledgements

Nothing springs fully formed from a void.

What I hope is that what I have written is worthy of those who have taught and worked with me over the years when this collection took form.

My time at the University of San Francisco was valuable time, not just from being able to work with talented writers both in and out of class, but also for affording me the opportunity to escape the realm of everyday work, to experience the texture of the place.

In addition to the university and those whom I knew and worked with while studying there, I recognize the contributions of my family and my friends to my developing view and memory of life on the Gulf Coast.

I must admit that my perspectives are not theirs but at the core I value the sense of diversity of experience and complexity of trying to express that experience to others.

The form of what I have written springs from that ground.

In this cycle, I've tried to remain authentic to the experiences of my life.

I am grateful for the time and care expressed by the
Others in my life;
wife, children,

my Afghan Hounds both here and departed,
Montana, Markey, Jolie, Niki, and Howl,

my parents, grandparents, and friends.

Front Cover: Chandhara's Rainbow Warrior (aka Howl) and the author's son taking a rest break on Howl's trip from the Chandhara Kennel in Maryland to live with the author in Fairhope, Al (11/2008). Howl's first trip in a car. *– photo by the author.*

Back Cover: Chandhara's Rainbow Warrior (Howl) and Jendar's Body of Evidence (Niki) with the author and his wife at their house in Wetumpka, AL (8/2011). *photo by Theresa Wayne.*

Contents...

- Cocobolo -

Foreword

I live in a house on the rim of an ancient impact crater. It is a special place, the land that is my bit of the rim. A holy place I think. The ground is dense with shocked quartz. Yesterday on the place we call the Point, the highest spot on this ridge, where we can hear gurgling water underground trickling down to the river at the foot of the rim, I found the shank of a broken arrowhead. It was lying under pines in the fine sand that forms the ground there. Made from white quartz, I wondered if it was a reject, discarded by the Indian craftsman when it broke while he worked it. Quartz is brittle. It might have never been completely formed. I ran my finger across the broken edge and it was smooth. I looked around the spot we call the Point. There were no signs of who he or she or they were; or when the arrow's shank was left or why. Or who or why three hollies are planted on the edge of the point; or if the lane worn across the ridgeline is a path or a road or a trail. Or when it was made and by whom. That is the way of life – mine anyway.

Place exists after the personalities are gone but is not immutable. Perhaps that's the thing that saddens me most about life. On the ridge, time is linear only as we experience it, and, when I think deeper about time, maybe not then. I'm not sure any more of time. Internal time is not the same as external. It is formed from thought and memory in the moment of existence and shapes what we perceive. Our experience of the present subsumes our reflections on the past and our reflections on the future, as we believe it might unfold within any moment of the present. In that sense, real time or experiential time is nonlinear. I used to tell my daughter that science was magic explained. I suspect that explanations are another form of magic.

One of the advantages of being southern is having internal permission for luxuriating in complex ambiguity, time shifting at will, nonlinear thought, love of the absurd (which is often the way of life), nostalgia, and an opposition to manufactured realms of reality found in tight well-formed fiction. Guns don't have to be used if present. Economy is not truth. Efficiency is actually a pretense when viewing life. This collection is southern, an organic unit, a piece of string. The first story is one end and the last is the other. The bits in the middle reflect the ends and all things in it are related.

It's only lately that I've truly come to appreciate the genius of *Losing Battles*.

I placed the shank of the broken arrow on the mantel in my house. The Indian who made it is dead but I can touch what he or she touched and because it still is, they still are, and in my mind they have a place and are not yet dead. Real stories don't begin and end...they start and stop. And sometimes start again.

Cliff Wayne
September 15, 2011

- Cocobolo -

Cocobolo

Me and Errol were sitting in Angelo's
drinking some whiskey one Saturday
afternoon. It was in the fall about midway
through the college football season and LSU
wasn't doing so well, that's why we were
just sitting at a table talking about hunting
instead of watching the TV. Errol liked to
drink Wild Turkey, not my favorite, and I
was drinking Old Forrester. We never really
agreed on much but I liked him so we got a
long. Me and him were in grade school
together all the way through high school.
He went on to college for a time, but me, I
was working for the city in the maintenance
department. He came back to town after a
couple of years. He did odd jobs around
town for folks.

We were sitting there talking about
whether or not it was right to use corn to
bait deer when these two guys at the bar
started talking in the middle of the football
game. One of them, the short one, said he
had been watching a cop show and it was
about this sliver of wood that broke off a

pool cue and drove its way into this guy's heart and killed him.

The other guy, a tall skinny one, said he thought that was a load of shit cause no sliver of wood could go through your skin like that.

The short guy said it could because it was cocobolo wood.

The skinny guy started laughing at the other one so hard he almost slipped off his bar stool. Said he never heard of anything called cocobolo and figured it was just made up for that damn TV show.

By that time, me and Errol were turned around in our chairs to see how things were going to turn out. Anytime two guys start getting into it about something in a bar you want to pay attention so you don't get mixed up in it by accident. Nothing like being shot or killed when you were just minding your own business.

Well, the short guy pulled out his cell phone punched in some stuff on it and told the skinny guy that cocobolo was a tree that got to be 50 or 60 feet high down in the rainforest and takes about 100 years to grow. Which is what made it rare. That's why average people never heard of it. And the reason it could have stabbed that guy through the heart is it was heavy and didn't absorb water. It didn't even float it was so dense. So a sliver of wood like that would be just like a nail going through that guys skin.

The skinny guy looked at the other one's cell phone and then gave it back. Everybody else in the bar looked back at the pool table and the rack of beat up cues lined up against the wall. It was a hard thing to sit there wanting to go look and see if those things had cocobolo wood on them but not wanting to look ignorant at the same time. That lasted about 30 seconds before we all piled into the back of Angelo's standing around the pool cues. Sure enough the cues had these dark wood inlays in them that might have been cocobolo wood. We didn't know since none of us had never seen it before. In the dark back there it was hard to see so we grabbed those pool cues and staggered outside in the sun so we could see 'em better.

Everybody wanted to know what color does the guy's cell phone say the cocobolo wood was. The skinny guy said according to the article on the phone it was a rosewood tree so it must be red but the short man with the phone said in the article it was all colors between red and dark brown. Some of the cues had a dark wood inlay on them but a bunch of them turned out to be just decaled or painted. It figured that Angelo's wouldn't have any high-end cues. Eddy, the new owner, was a cheap sumbitch.

About that time the cops showed up. A group of guys standing around behind Angelo's holding pool cues and drinking wasn't the sort of thing that looked innocent. I reckon somebody around there must have called the cops when they saw us piling out of the door with those cue sticks. A couple of the cops in St. Helena, like that Eddie Ackerbacker for one, were pricks so we went back inside before they arrested us for just being outside the bar with our drinks.

When we got back inside, I asked Errol if he'd ever heard of cocobolo wood before. He was a smart guy, smarter than me, but he said he never had. Errol said he had an uncle that had a custom cue he played with. Carried it in a special aluminum Halliburton case to shoot pool in different bars. He said it probably had that cocobolo wood. But it cost too much for his uncle to have been hitting anybody with it so hard it would break and make a sliver of that wood go into somebody's heart. More than likely his uncle would have just used a bar stool to beat 'em to death.

We decided that cop show on TV was full of crap. Those writers didn't know shit about playing pool.

- Cocobolo -

M. Vicknair Reads
Tonight At 6

On Thursday nights in a room above a boutique bookstore on the Gulf Coast, writers on the independent book circuit would come to read from their just published books hoping to find a reader or stimulate a sale or two. The crowd in the room varied with the season.

The bookstore was in a village that perched on the eastern bluff of a bay and winter residents from Canada or Ohio or Michigan or some other cold winter place would flesh out the full time crowd of retired residents. In summer, after the winter residents re-migrated, a sprinkling of tourists escaping the inland heat for a week or a month of beach time and Gulf air might fill a few of the empty chairs in the upstairs room.

On a June evening, when heat and humidity had driven everyone inside for air-conditioning, Melissa Vicknair sat behind a table in the room above the bookstore and prepared to read a section from her first novel, _No Way Home_. She adjusted her glasses on the bridge of her nose and tucked a curl of dark hair back in place

7

behind her ear while Bill Winston, the store manager, introduced her to the small group in the room and read a few critical comments about her work.

"*No Way Home*, set in 1930's Istanbul, is Melissa's first novel and it has garnered a wealth of positive reviews from all over the country. She says it had begun as a mystery novel but quickly morphed on her into a piece about a woman rebuilding her life after a scandalous love affair with a Persian merchant. Melissa grew up over in Louisiana near New Orleans but currently lives in San Francisco."

She was half listening to Bill as she scanned the room. Instead of books, paintings with little business cards tucked in the bottom right corners of the frames covered the walls. Facing her was a large painting four feet high and five feet long of 3 Guernsey cows under an oak grazing in a pasture. Except for the golden cows at its center, it was dark green and brown. The rest of the paintings in the room were pelicans, palm trees, and magnolias. All were for sale.

The painting of the cows pulled on her. She studied it for the source of why.

It wasn't the cows. They were ok. Something else was unordinary about it.

The style was primitive, cows looking out of the canvas with flat empty eyes. Primitive art was not usually her interest but she could accept it as a form of naïve expression. At least it seemed honest.

Probably some little grandmother working in her dining room painted it. Converted her dining room into some sort of studio after her husband died and the grandmother would work in there all day painting this piece about cows in her dead uncle's pasture - a childhood memory.

Or she might have cows. They might be her cows in her pasture and each one would have a name. Bessy, Maude, and Judy. Three sister cows spending an afternoon in the pasture watching the artist work at her easel. They would stop and stare and resume ruminating on the strange scene of the woman from the big house working behind the canvas. Or man. But she thought not. It didn't have a man's perspective. Sometimes she wondered why she would think such a thing, this wasn't the first time, and forming judgments like that disturbed her. It might be a man in the pasture painting the cows, but not really. She was sure it was a woman.

It was so large. Melissa could not imagine where anyone would hang it. Or, why would they buy it in the first place. She laughed out loud imagining it suspended on a wall behind a sofa in a living room. Three sister cows looking out on a dinner party.

A woman at the back of the room coughed.

Melissa turned from the painting to the faces of the crowd.

Their eyes fixed on her, plastic wine glasses perched politely on paper napkins in their palms, waiting for the beginning of her reading. Bill had already stepped away from the podium and was sitting in the chair beside her.

Flustered, Melissa fumbled for her book, stood, and thanked Bill for his warm introduction and kind words. "Tonight, I'm going to begin reading from the opening scene of the piece."

Her agent told her it was a wonderful opening, introduced the protagonist, Julie, and set the scene, an archaeology dig outside of Istanbul with an economy of expression. She hoped they would enjoy the exotic location.

Her friends said it made them feel as if they had traveled somewhere.

She read for ten minutes.

In a pause before the section where Julie would walk into an Istanbul cafe and meet her lover, Melissa noted silence in the room. She looked up in time to see a woman in the second row yawn politely behind her hand.

Melissa picked up her water bottle and took a sip to give herself time to think.

Maybe she would read from a different scene, the beginning of the breakup, perhaps. Her agent told her it conveyed a compelling sense of the emotional weight that the protagonist carried in the piece, nicely setting up the climax of her decision to return to America.

She put the water bottle down and plunged into the breakup scene.

For five minutes, Melissa read through muffled coughs and rustling noises from clothes as bodies shifted positions in plastic chairs. Before the end of her scheduled time, she closed the book and forced a smile for the blank faces.

Disinterest, it happened.

She was learning to cope and always hoped the next bookstore audience would enjoy it more, sigh or smile or laugh, anything but sit so uncomfortably. She gripped her water bottle to steady her hands and told the group, "Well. There's a little time left for questions and answers. Did anyone have any questions?"

In the center of the room, she spotted a hand raised shoulder high. It belonged to a thin little woman, perm'd white hair, and turquoise flowered blouse.

"Yes, ma'm?"

"Have you written any cook books?"

"Cook books?" That was a first. "No. I can't say that I have."

The little woman's smile closed.

Quick to recover, Melissa said, "I do recall my mother collecting a bunch of her recipes one time for the Junior League. That was back a few years. I was in high school at the time. We had just moved from Dutch Bayou to Baton Rouge and they were coming out with an update of *River Road Recipes.*"

She saw a few in the crowd lean a fraction closer to her. "You know of that cookbook?"

The crowd murmured and a few oh yeses stood out, so she dove into the story.

"My momma had a recipe for chicken andouille that she submitted and then another one for a lemon meringue pie. It was a custard pie though. Not an icebox like most everybody makes. She spent weeks trying to decide on what recipes to submit. She asked me what I thought, but I didn't have any idea. I told her, 'Momma, all your cooking is good. Just pick one. Close your eyes and pull one out of your recipe box.'

"But Momma knew where her recipes were in that box even with her eyes closed. So what she did was she opened her box and had me close my eyes and pick one. So I did. And what I picked out was a recipe for a Frito pie. Y'all remember those?"

Heads in the crowd nodded slightly like trees in a breeze.

"She said, 'Oh my, that just won't do. You have to pick another.' So I did and out came a recipe for a paprika beef roll. She didn't like that either. Finally, after about five tries I pulled out the recipes for chicken andouille and lemon meringue pie. And that's how they got in *River Road Recipes* back then."

She glanced around the room at the faces with eyes finally focused on her.

"Anybody here know what andouille is?"

Two or three hands went up.

"Well, for those of you who don't, andouille is a pork sausage, like ham actually. It has chunks of ham, fat, and some spices. If you ever bought any from a store, that's not it. It's not what they sell you in the stores. If you want real andouille, you have to travel to the towns up the river from New Orleans about twenty or thirty miles. That was called the German Coast when my parents were growing up. That's where I'm from. And that's where andouille came from."

The woman in a pink pants suit raised her hand and interrupted, "I thought it was Cajun sausage."

"People say it's Cajun but that's marketing. The way they throw Cajun around now, it doesn't mean anything. They do that to everything in Louisiana. Momma says when she was growing up everybody used Creole the same way. Creole was high class New Orleans cooking. Everything was Creole in her day."

The woman in the pink pants suit said, "I love Creole cooking," and the rest of the room twittered, amused at her interruption.

"Well, it's not Creole either. It's from the German coast. I bet you never heard of that, have you.

"Forty years before Acadians got to Louisiana, there was a German Coast on the river. My Momma says that when she was a girl, the Cajuns mostly lived west of the Atchafalaya swamp in a place everybody called Acadiana. You've heard of Evangeline by Hawthorne? That's where it was. And the Creoles were mostly over on the east side around New Orleans. It stayed like that until my Momma was in college and they built the interstate across the swamp. After that you could drive across the state in two and a half hours instead of it taking all day to drive north around the swamp. I don't think there's any real Acadiana left anymore. It's all just marketing. And the German Coast has gone too. Nobody even remembers it existed anymore."

She felt the crowd stirring, swishing cloth from shifting bottoms restless in the plastic chairs. "That's enough of my soapbox. I hope I didn't scare anybody," and all of them laughed with her for a polite intermission in tension.

She rubbed her thumb across the spine of her book and stared at the painting of cows in a pasture. She could see Dutch Bayou as foreign to the world as Istanbul, as lost as Constantinople. A lost place, fading under Istanbul's layerings of new lives and new accounts of how the earth was formed with people wandering on streets above it all never knowing that beneath them lay a forgotten city, another land that came before what they knew.

"There used to be a wonderful restaurant down the River Road from Dutch Bayou where I grew up named Rousells'. When I was a little girl, great grandmother used to tell me stories about her mamma riding out from New Orleans in a buggy when she was a young woman to eat at that restaurant. That's where she met my great-great-grandfather, when it was still on the River Road. When the only road out of New Orleans was the River Road.

"My great-grandmother said Rousells' had a wonderful old live oak beside it and in the evening, the breeze would come in off the river and cool everything. That's before the levees were high like they are now.

"When I was very young, I remember seeing the old wooden building where the original restaurant was. It was right in a hairpin bend of the road, right by the river. It's been torn down.

"When they built the Airline Highway between New Orleans and Baton Rouge, Momma said everything started moving away from the river. Even Rousells'. Instead of following the high ground of the riverbank, it cut straight across the land and swamp on a berm of dirt. Now it's the interstate highway north of town pulls people even farther from the river."

A woman in the back raised her hand and asked, "What is chicken andouille? Is it like a fricassee?"

Melissa closed her novel.

"Oh no. Basically it's a chicken soup cooked with andouille. Momma told me one time that the original recipe was like an old German chicken and garlic sausage soup. Momma would serve hers with a scoop of white rice, not too much rice. The combination of flavors is just wonderful. But don't put vegetables in it. It's not a vegetable soup. And don't make it with a roux. Momma never made hers with a roux. Some do but not Momma. That would be a gumbo. That's what people in Louisiana do now to everything, but I don't think that's authentic."

The little woman asked, "Do you have a copy of the recipes in your new book?"

"No, I don't."

"That's a shame. They sound wonderful."

"I'm sure you can find them in a cookbook somewhere."

A woman in the middle of the group said, "You know, I saw a writer on TV yesterday morning and she said that she puts recipes in her mystery books. You should try it."

Melissa made her lips smile and her voice say, "Maybe I will."

Bill Winston half stood and leaned toward the mic, "We have several copies of *River Road Recipes* on hand downstairs for those of you who would like to purchase a copy. It's one of our perennial favorites."

The crowd broke into murmured conversations about favorite cookbooks.

"Are there any other questions for Ms. Vicknair?" The hum in the room slowed. "Well, we would like to thank Ms. Vicknair for coming all the way over from San Francisco to read from her new novel tonight. If any of you would like to purchase a copy of her book, I'm certain that she'd be pleased to sign it for you."

With that, there was polite applause and the room emptied, each person taking their plastic wine glass with them.

Melissa placed her novel inside her bag and took another look at the painting of the cows. The perspective of it skewed with the fence in the background, the same height going left to right even though it was receding.

She asked Bill, "Who painted the cows?"

"Susan Morse. She's a local artist. Do you like it?"

"I'm not sure, really. It's not the sort of thing I usually find interesting. Not that it's not done well."

Melissa's eye tracked the top line of the distorted fence.

"Susan is one our folk artists. When she got back from New York, that's where she went to university, she said she had to do something real. So she started doing pieces like this. Said it was damned hard to do." He glanced at her, "Pardon me."

"I don't know anything about art. Seems like folk art would be the easiest thing. Just get a brush and start painting."

"I wouldn't know, myself. I'm not an artist. She says civilization keeps leaking out of your fingertips though. It ruins the art."

"That's interesting."

"She's a character alright. Says the trick is to turn off the forms in her head while she's working so she can see."

When they reached the door Bill turned out the light and closed the door to the room. "Be careful on these old stairs. They're steep."

"I will," she smiled politely in the dim. "I heard a story once about a chef who was traveling through Spain. When he came upon a fantastic dish, he had to have the recipe. So he went back to the kitchen and told the old woman who was cooking that he was a world famous chef and asked if he could have her recipe. Said it was the most wonderful dish he had eaten in a month. She sighed and told him she could not tell him. She told him, 'a kitchen does not travel.' And then she told him, 'You must eat it where it is born.' "

"That's a wonderful story," Bill followed behind her and she couldn't see his face to tell if he was only being polite. Undeserved politeness was a southern flaw she had forgotten about.

At the bottom of the stairs, she told Bill Winston that she wanted to buy the painting of the cows. Could he ship it to her address in San Francisco?

Bill smiled big and said that it would be no trouble at all. Susan would be thrilled to know that her painting was going to San

Francisco. He asked where she was going to hang it.

Melissa stepped from the stairs to the tiled floor. "I haven't thought that far ahead yet," and smiled. She had a small apartment in a house near Geary. "I don't really know where I'll put it. But that's ok."

- Cocobolo-

Chicken Andouille

By M. Vicknair

1 large onion, diced
2 tablespoons of butter, unsalted
1 tablespoons of olive oil
10 cups of chicken stock
3/4 lb. of Andouille sausage, cut into 1/2-inch thick rounds
2 cups of chicken meat, coarsely chopped and cooked
Salt and pepper, to taste

In a heavy-bottomed, 6-quart saucepan, cook the onions in the butter and oil over moderate heat, stirring frequently, for 3-5 minutes, or until onions are translucent.

Add sausage and cook until the fat melts.

Add the chicken, the chicken stock, and seasoning, then bring it to a boil over high heat.

After the stock boils for about 3 minutes, reduce the heat to low and simmer for at least 10 - 15 more minutes.

Serve over a scoop of rice.

Somewhere Nobody
Usually Goes

In the dead time between late night and early morning, the bartender propped open the door of Angelo's to let in some fresh air while he cleaned up. It was humid air, warm off the Gulf and moved over land like breath, carried the musk of salt marsh and damp bark rot into Angelo's sweet ferment of spilled whisky and beer.

The bartender turned off the jukebox and from Angelo's insides a voice was saying, "The thing about freaky relationships is they're only good when you ain't in em. Like Martha, that's a memory."

A little man was sitting on a barstool telling stories while he drank. Other than the bartender and a waitress, he was the only one left in the place. "After a couple of months, we broke up but it seems like a year. Never knew what crazy assed thing she'd do next. How about you?"

The bartender stopped sweeping and looked up. "What?"

"You had any freaky women."

"No, man." The bartender went back to sweeping. "I keep it straight and level."

The little man laughed. "Shit, you ain't lived 'til you had a woman scare the hell out of you. I was tempted to lock up the kitchen knives when that one stayed over."

"Why don't you finish off that beer and go home. I want to close up."

"Yeah, yeah." The little man emptied the mug and staggered off the barstool.

The bartender walked over to the front door. "You need a cab?"

"I'm walkin'."

"Be careful out there."

"Bullshit." The little man stumbled out the door and tripped down the sidewalk past the streetlight.

The bartender turned off the neon Angelo's sign and locked up.

Julie was standing at the bar with her tray of empties. "I thought the little prick would never leave." She was wearing her sequined baby blue halter-top, jeans, and cowboy boots. She glittered under the bar lights.

"He didn't have anywhere to go. Kept talking about Mike's all night. They don't let him go in there anymore." The bartender began rinsing glasses and mugs. "So, what about you. You got any plans tomorrow?"

"I always got plans. I just can't afford the plane ticket."

"Where you planning on going?"

"Hawaii."

"I never wanted to go to Hawaii."

"You're kiddin' me. Everybody wants to go to Hawaii."

"Never had the desire."

"Where would you go then? If you could go anywhere in the world."

He flipped the bar rag over his shoulder and set the rinsed mugs and glasses in the washer. "I think I would go somewhere nobody usually goes."

"Like where?"

"I was watching a show last week and they were in Romania exploring the ruins of Dracula's castles. I think I'd like to see that."

"You're shittin' me."

"No. Really."

"Dracula was a vampire."

"Not the character." He grinned at her. "The real Dracula."

"I know you're lying now." She sat on a barstool and lit up a cigarette, one long leg crossed over the top of the other. "Dracula was a movie. Or are you talking about the Dafoe guy who was in that other vampire movie."

"You never heard the real story of Dracula?"

"Stop." She held her hand up at him. She had long thin fingers and her palms were worn tough. "That's enough."

"His name was Vlad."

"Stop it right now. You're beginning to scare me with all that vampire talk. You know I got to walk through the dark to get to my house."

"He wasn't a vampire. He was a prince."

"I don't want to hear no more about it. Seeing Dracula's castle is no place to want to go at 2AM in the morning."

He threw the towel into the hamper. "Ok. No more Dracula talk."

"I never cared much for those Anne Rice stories anyway."

"I never read 'em."

"You're kidding me. You never read *Interview With a Vampire*? The Vampire Lestad?"

"No. You?"

"Everybody's read Ann Rice. I thought you said you liked to read."

"I read different things."

"Like what."

He leaned forward on the bar. "Last week I read *The Wine of Youth.*"

"Never heard of it."

"It's a collection of stories by a guy named Fante."

"Never heard of him. You ought to read *Interview of a Vampire.*"

"Interview With the Vampire."

"Whatever.... You ought to read it so you can say you liked it or not."

"Maybe I will."

"Especially if you want to go see Dracula's castle. Sounds to me like it might be something you'd like."

"Might be."

He leaned on his elbows and watched the girl. She was intense. Exhaling cigarette smoke, her eyes narrowed into mascara slits staring at him.

"So, what's that Fante guy write about?"

"People, like his family and himself. You wouldn't like it."

"Why not?"

"Some of his descriptions are crude."

"How do you know I wouldn't like it?"

He saw her jaw clench hard enough for the muscles in it to turn into knots. "Guess I don't."

"Where's he from?"

"His parents were Italian but he grew up in Colorado. During the depression, he moved to California."

"So, these are old stories."

"Not too old."

"The depression was a hundred years ago. That's history."

"It's not like watching a black and white movie."

She ground out her cigarette. "You bring it in and I'll read it."

"I'll do that."

"And I'll bring you *Interview of a Vampire*."

"It's a deal. Want a beer?"

"Sure. I'm not sleepy yet. That's the thing about working late. Once I get past 2 o'clock, I'm tired but I can't go to sleep."

He pulled a tap handle and drew her beer.

She lit a second cigarette and held it between her fingers. She had high gloss blood red polished fingernails.

"So why was it you moved back to this crappy town?"

"It's complicated."

"I wouldn't have. I'd done whatever it took to stay gone. You were in L.A."

"The last couple of years, it was like having cancer."

"What kind of cancer."

"Soul cancer."

She frowned. "You think strange. You know that? Anybody ever tell you that? Least you made it to California."

"Never made it to Hawaii though."

She said nothing and smoked the cigarette.

He drew a glass for himself and held it toward her. "Good times." Then he frowned. "People say stupid things when they're holding a drink."

She tapped her glass on his. "It's not stupid. It's a blessing. Good times."

"A blessing. So this would be like a church?"

"A temple."

"And you would be the priestess." He bowed his head to her in mock adoration, lost his balance, and splashed beer onto the bar top.

She laughed at him. "And you could be my temple slave."

"I'd rather be a god."

"You don't act like a god."

"What's a god act like?"

She sipped beer and looked at him. "I don't know. I guess they have supernatural powers."

"How's this?" He shouted, "Rain," and pointed at the sky.

She laughed at him, tilting her chin up to reveal her throat, slender, naked, and brown until a long rumbling thunder made her eyes widen and her laughing stop.

"How'd you do that?"

"I'm a god."

"You shouldn't say things like that. It's not right." She set her glass on the bar and stood up. "I need to be getting home."

"Oh come on, I was just kidding around." He pointed at the TV perched on a stand in a far corner of the room. "It's on the local weather channel. I've been watching a thunderstorm head this way."

She glanced at the TV and then turned back to the bar, reaching her hand over it, groping for her purse. "Yeah, well I don't want to have to walk home in the rain."

"It's already raining."

He went over and opened the back door. The rain was heavy coming off the roof. "After we finish the beers, I'll give you a ride."

"On your bike?"

"I have the old Camaro."

"That car your brother had?"

"It's a classic."

She stood in the open door while rain splattered the silver capped toe tips of her boots. "I could wait a little longer."

"Good. At least we can finish our beers."

They went back to the bar and she settled again on the barstool.

He passed her a pasteboard coaster for her glass. "You don't want me to be a god, huh?"

"Ok, that's just freaky talk, you know."

"Like talking about vampires?"

"Any of that unnatural shit. At 2 AM anything unnatural is freaky."

"During the day, it's ok?"

"During the day, you can see." She swirled the beer in her glass. "And vampires don't come out during the day."

"Werewolves either."

"There you go again."

"Or Frankenstein."

"Frankenstein could be in the day. Remember when he met that little girl out in the woods. That was in the day."

"I never liked that part."

"He was a monster. That's different from vampires and werewolves. They're supernatural creatures."

"Maybe I could be a demigod."

"What's a demigod do?"

"That's like Hercules."

"That's ok." She drank some of her beer. "Can you do something strong?"

"No. But I have other powers."

"I see." She smiled into her glass. "I'm not even going to ask what those are. How did you get to be a demigod?"

"Ah, that's a good one. Ummm..." he stalled. "A demigod has one parent that's a mortal and one that's a god."

"Like Jesus."

"I was thinking of Hercules. His dad was Zeus and his mother was a woman."

"I don't think either one of your parents was a god."

"My dad thought he was."

"All dads think they are." She finished her beer and put the empty glass on the bar. "I need to get home. I have to help momma get the kids ready for school in a couple of hours."

"Sure." He took her glass, rinsed it, and placed it in the washer.

She got off the barstool. "I'm living with her now. I got a restraining order on Ricky."

"That's good. How're your kids." He rinsed his own glass and put it in the washer.

"Fine. My boy is in first grade. Learning his numbers."

"What about Hannah." He turned on the washer, looked one last time around the room, and turned off the TV with the remote.

"She's doing ok. She's quiet most of the time. Hardly know she's in the room."

"How old is she now?" He crossed the room with her to the back door.

"She's twelve."

"Fourth grade?"

"Mmhm, fifth. She likes to read but she doesn't pay attention in class."

She waited under the overhang while he set the burglar alarm and locked the door. Arms crossed tight over her breasts, rain splatter droplets collected on the fine hairs of her skin.

She teased him, "Since you started it, why don't you make it stop raining."

He looked into the rain and shouted, "Stop."

She laughed and stepped under his umbrella ready to run to the garage where he kept the Camaro.

The rain stopped.

Her eyes widened and stared at him. "How'd you do that?"

He collapsed the umbrella and shook off the water.

"Lucky I guess."

She walked to the garage without talking and waited for him to back the Camaro into the road. Gleaming black and invisible in the dark the Camaro rumbled and rolled out of the garage. He blipped the accelerator. The exhaust ripped the air and trembled the earth.

He grinned at her from behind the windshield and shouted, "Just like high school."

Her hand gripped the door handle. She looked in at him and shouted, "I'm going to walk."

He pressed a button and lowered the passenger window.

"What?"

"I'm going to walk."

He reached across and opened her door. "Com'on, I got the car out and everything," but she was already on the sidewalk and hurrying into the safe dark of her mother's unlit neighborhood.

He shouted after her, "I'm not a vampire."

Her voice came back, "What are you then?"

"I'm really a prince."

From the dark Julie shouted, "That's what they all say."

The bartender turned off the engine, listened to her high-pitched laughter and the hard sound of her boots running away into the black. He reached over to close the passenger door and restarted the car.

"What a freak," and he burned rubber all the way from Angelo's back across the railroad tracks.

- Cocobolo -

Barista

Marlene Englade held a stainless steel pot under the steam spigot and frothed a cup of milk. Every morning from 7 to 10, her hands moved in the routine of grind the beans, load the espresso machine, froth the milk, pour, serve, and clean.

While her hands worked, she gazed at a spot on the wallpaper by her counter. A bit of splashed coffee from a spilled latte, she pretended she saw the Alps inside it. All morning while she made coffee, she watched the stain and imagined living in the Alps.

She had never been to the Alps or even out of Louisiana, but Ms. Jaubert, her 8th grade history teacher had. Every summer, Ms. Jaubert traveled from New Orleans to Austria and spent a month visiting a friend from college. She brought back post cards and calendars. She had glossy 8 1/2 by 11 photographs that she took while hiking in the mountains. Ms. Jaubert stuck them on the walls in her classroom and told stories of traveling in Europe. Ms. Jaubert told stories about drinking espresso in Vienna.

She said that Austria was beautiful and she loved the Alps. She made them read Heidi and at Christmas, she showed them the movie with Shirley Temple in it even though she admitted it was set in Switzerland not Austria, but at least it was the Alps. Everybody in class thought it was stupid but after 8th grade, Marlene wanted to live in the Alps. She never told anyone. Now she was 18.

A customer on the other side of the counter called out, "Light on the foam."

She nodded and echoed, "Light foam."

Marlene poured a double shot of espresso into a heavy ceramic cup of hot milk and traced a tulip pattern with steamed milk on the top of the brown tinged black espresso. That was her signature and dropped a spoonful of foam over the design.

Marlene slid the finished cup across the counter top. "Latte, light foam."

Before the hands could reach across for the cup, she turned to clean the machine for the next round. She removed the metal basket that held the spent grounds and rapped it against a can under the counter. Sometimes she poked the dislodged disk of compressed grounds with her finger to see how much pressure it took to change them from a black puck into dust. The disk would hold until overwhelmed it collapsed into powder. She told Francine it was stupid but she liked watching something that was solid in one-minute collapse to dust in the next.

She slid the can of used grounds back under the counter.

Every afternoon a raggedy man came to collect the spent grounds. He said it was for his compost; rough beard, tee shirt, and old jeans. In winter, he wore a green army field jacket. If it was raining, he added a wide brimmed hat, but no umbrella. He said he didn't like umbrellas. Hats worked better.

When he came in the shop, he didn't talk other than to say Hey. But if she got him talking about his compost pile he wouldn't shut up. Sometimes, just to get him started, she asked him, "Why does rotten food make dirt?"

Every time she did, he said it wasn't rotting food. It was decomposing. He talked about bacteria cultures and optimum temperatures until she walked away. He was a freak. He never figured out that she didn't care. It was her game to kill time. Eventually he'd drift out carrying his bucket of used up grounds and come back the next day when they would do the same thing again.

Francine who worked the register said he was a friend of Mr. Guidry, the owner. Francine said she thought they were in the army together. Marlene imagined they were in Viet Nam, smoking ganja and sneaking around in the jungle, like *Apocalypse Now*. Going up the Mekong on jungle boats, stoned. But she wasn't sure if they were old enough to be in that war. They had grey hair but *Apocalypse Now* was farther back. Maybe it was another war. One of the desert wars like in *Three Kings* stealing hordes of gold. She preferred imagining the jungle wars though with rain and wet and usually stayed with that. She understood wet not desert.

The worms in his compost must be freaked on caffeine and she laughed every time she added fresh grounds for another espresso knowing where they would end up. Worms strung out on espresso beans must make good composters, working their butts off. One time she asked him if it was ok for the worms to eat so much caffeine but he just looked at her as if she was a kook or something. She didn't ask again.

He was strange but she didn't believe he was dangerous.

She rinsed and wiped the espresso machine at the end of the morning crush. It was a two station Gaggia Luxus, chrome and brass with the optional eagle crested Luxus dome. It was a work of art and she made it gleam. That was her morning.

At 10, she took off her barista apron, told Francine she was going on break, and stepped outside the shop. Mr. Guidry didn't want them standing by the shop when they were on break so she walked around the corner and down an alley to an upended plastic carton. No smoking in the shop so she and Francine made the end of the alley their break room. She had fifteen minutes. She pulled out a cigarette and lit up.

"Hey girl." It was jerk Bobby from the pet store next door. "You got my seat." He was already smoking as he walked down the alley, knit cap pulled down over his floppy head, baggy pants dragging cuffs on the asphalt sounding scuff swipe every time he took a step.

"I don't see your name on it." She flipped him off and he grinned.

"What're you doing today?"

"Same thing I do every morning, Pinky."

"Yeah. Well, Stimpy, I don't think the world is worth taking over."

"You're in a pissy mood. And it's Brain not Stimpy. You got the wrong cartoon."

Bobby leaned his back into the wall and slid down until he was crouched tight and curled over his knees, burning cigarette dangling from his fingertips. "Word is they're going to layoff tomorrow."

"So. Get another sucky job." She blew smoke at him and he leaned into the bricks behind him. She never cut Bobby any slack. She couldn't. He was a goof. Give him a break and he'd take everything she had. That's the way his kind were, leaches.

"That's not the point." He blew a cloud back at her. "It's getting beat down. That's the friggin' point."

"Beat down's nothing new for you." He didn't come back with anything and Marlene watched him a minute before asking, "What makes you think they're going to cut you loose?"

"Everybody else's been there longer. They got their little preppy club."

Bobby was a whiner, which was something else she didn't like about him.

"You know how it is." He took a last drag on his cigarette, then flipped the burned out butt down the center of the alley, and said, "Three points. Got another smoke?"

"Hell no." She lied. She had an extra pack in her bag, but you couldn't let him freeload. Besides, he needed to cut back. She was really doing him a favor. If you can't afford 'em you shouldn't smoke 'em. That's what her dad used to say.

Bobby leaned his head over sideways for a second and then pointed at her chest, "What's that?"

She glanced down at breastbone skin not covered by her Guidry's Coffee shirt. "My new tattoo."

"What is it?" He craned his neck toward her trying to see.

"Back, freak." She shoved him, "It's my dragon." She pulled the collar aside so that he could see a bit of the wing where it rose on her right shoulder. "It's like my avatar."

"Damn, girl. How big is it?"

"It's big."

"Sick. How many colors?"

"Six. The body is sort of a forest green with red accents on the tips of the scales.

Then there's some blue outlining and some yellow. The eyes are yellow."

"That's only four."

"There's also brown and a bit of pink on the wings. It's a European. They have wings. Chinese dragons don't have wings."

"I never could get into that fantasy shit."

She squeezed her eyelids until he disappeared black. He didn't know shit about DnD. He enjoyed being stupid so she let him run on.

"You guys played that crap in high school and I just never got it."

She straightened her shirt, smoothed the cloth until it returned to its shape. "You have to learn the rules, you know." He always talked about when they were in high school but she didn't even remember who he was. Sometimes she wondered if he had gone or if he was fakin' to get close. "Even magic's got limits."

"I'm not saying there's anything wrong with it. I just don't get it. You guys, sitting around outside the cafeteria, huddled up in your little group."

"Yeah, well I don't remember you."

"Cold, baby." He gave her that stupid fist salute with his thumb and little finger sticking out. Bullshit artist, he learned that watching TV.

"I don't like thinking about high school much less talking about it every damn day. You thought about what you're going to do if they cut you?"

"My bro lives out in L.A. I think I might," he trailed off at that point and made a vague motion at the end of the alley.

"So you got no idea."

"I just play it as it comes." He grinned like he wasn't scared. "You ought to drop this joint and come out with me."

"That ain't my idea of a lifestyle improvement." She squinted at him, making him blur out between her eyelashes. "My dad used to say once you leave you can never go back."

"Bullshit." He sat his butt on the concrete and uncoiled his legs. "This ain't nowhere special."

She ground her cigarette butt into the black spot on the brick next to her. "I got to get back. Good luck tomorrow. If I don't see you again, I'll know what happened."

She walked down the alley to the coffee shop. Before she rounded the corner, she turned and shouted, "Send me a card from L.A." Thank god she'd never see him again. He pissed her off every morning at break. And he never did get it. She stepped back inside the coffee shop, Francine's turn for a smoke.

Marlene wrapped the barista apron around her waist and stood behind the counter while Francine hurried outside to take her place on the upended carton. The next surge of work would be prep for the dinner rush; clean the counters, refill the milk and cream containers, empty the trash containers.

Marlene looked for the latte stain on the wall by the Luxus but it was gone. Francine must have cleaned it. Marlene flipped a splash of coffee on the wall before she asked the next customer what he wanted.

At 6AM, Marlene Englade stood in front of Guidry's waiting for Francine to show with the key to the door. Francine was late. Francine was always late so it wasn't anything new. Francine dropped her kids off at her mother's on the way in and let her mom get them fed and on the bus for school. That's the way Francine's mother told it. Marlene didn't want kids. She liked things the way they were. Some things.

Marlene smoked a cigarette while she waited. Her mother said she smoked too much. Whenever she went over to the house she tried not to smoke just to avoid the misery of listening to her mother bitch. Every time she walked in the front door her mother would hug her and then say she smelled like cigarettes. At least she didn't drink. Hard liquor.

She looked at her watch. 6:15. Francine should be here in a minute. She flipped the cigarette butt into the parking lot before Francine drove up. She didn't want to listen to a bunch of talk about smoking in front of the coffee shop. How would Guidry know it was her anyway unless Francine said?

At 6:17 Francine parked her car in the lot and came running, door keys in her hand, purse bouncing on its shoulder strap. She sounded like a circus animal, a circus horse wearing silver bells, quarters and dimes and makeup kits slapping around inside the purse. "Sorry," Francine called from across the lot. "The kids were hell this morning. Couldn't get them up. Jeff couldn't find his shoes. Every night I tell him to put them in the same place so he can find him." She said the same thing every morning.

"That's ok. I think I still have time to get the station ready." Since Francine was always late, Marline always did her prep work at night before they left. But wouldn't tell Francine, better to keep the pressure on. Marlene didn't want to be a store manager. If she were late, no one would care. Better to have 15 minutes of peace in the morning before hell than drop in after the start of it. Once behind you could never get caught up, that's what her dad used to say.

Marlene Englade held the stainless steel pot under the steam spigot and frothed a cup of milk. From 7 to 10, her hands moved in the routine of grind the beans, load the espresso machine, froth the milk, pour, serve, and clean. While her hands worked, she gazed at the spot on the wallpaper by her counter. The bit of splashed coffee she put there each morning. She imagined the Alps inside it. All morning while she made coffee, she watched the stain and imagined living in the Alps.

A customer on the other side of the counter called out, "Light foam."

She nodded and echoed, "Light foam."

Marlene poured a double shot of espresso into a heavy ceramic cup of hot milk and traced her signature tulip pattern with steamed milk on the top of the brown tinged black espresso. Dropped a spoonful of foam over the design, Marlene slid the finished cup across the counter top. "Latte, light foam."

Before the hands could reach to take the cup, she turned to clean the machine for the next round. She removed the metal basket that held the spent grounds and rapped it against a can under the counter. On a good morning, she would do that a hundred times, on a bad morning, maybe twenty.

At 10, she took off her barista apron, told Francine she was going on break, stepped outside the shop, and around the corner to the upended plastic carton at the end of the alley. Fifteen minutes to smoke.

No jerk Bobby came scuffing down the alley. He was gone. She leaned back into the brick and relaxed. First time in six months she didn't have to play chitchat during break. That was when he started at the pet store. None of the others in that joint smoked. Cigarettes anyway, she didn't know them. They were high school kids. She didn't know what they smoked. Bobby was probably at home watching game shows. He was a slacker. He wouldn't be going to L.A. even if his brother lived there. He was too scared. It was like her dad said, "Once you leave you can never go back."

It was a crappy pet store. She went in there one time to get some meds for her Betta and they didn't have shit. She always went to a store in Kenner. They had good fish, exotic Bettas and good meds. Not the stuff the chain stores sold. When a fish got sick you had to treat it right then or you'd lose it. That's the only reason why she went in there that time. She lost a few Bettas when she started with them but the last couple of years she hadn't lost any. She never went to that pet store again. Bobby was lucky he lasted as long as he did. She didn't know anybody who shopped there, unless they had pets for their kids. People who had pets for kids didn't really care. The animal was entertainment. Buy another when it died. She knew plenty of people who were that way. They might as well get them stuffed animals.

Marlene started a second cigarette.

Time moved slower without yakking Bobby. In the alley, it was quiet. The cinder block walls blocked the noise from the street and kept the sun out. Early spring and the shadows kept the air cool. She should have brought her long sleeved shirt out.

She ground her cigarette butt into the black spot on the brick next to her. Maybe tomorrow she would bring a book and a windbreaker.

Inside Guidry's, Marlene wrapped the barista apron around her waist and stood behind the counter while Francine hurried outside to take her place on the upended carton. The next surge was prep for the dinner rush. Clean the counters, refill the milk and cream containers, and empty the trash containers.

Marlene looked for the latte stain on the wall by the Luxus but it was gone. Francine cleaned it off the wall every morning. Marlene splashed coffee on the wall to form a silhouette of the Matterhorn. Guidry didn't let them stick pictures on the wall.

Barista

- Cocobolo

Oak Man Dog

The man and his dog would come by my house every morning at 9, then later at noon, and a third time at dusk, whatever time that happened to be. I could hear them coming down the street by the barking dogs through the neighborhood. There's a Schnauzer across the street from where the man lived that started barking when they stepped out the front door, a few rouw-rouw sounds and then it stopped because it loved the man's dog.

I didn't want a Schnauzer myself. I had a cat, a black one my dad called Smartass. He said he named it Smartass because the cat disappeared every time he came in the room. I called it Roger. Dad said, "That's not a cat name," but I called it Roger anyway. Roger was afraid of my dad sending it to the pound. They kill cats at the pound. I'd be afraid too, of dying like that. Cats, like everybody, want to live as long as they can.

Sometimes the man ran behind his dog but most times they walked, especially in the summer. In summer, the air is so humid it drips water and the heat can suffocate you. My mom said that's what you get living on the Gulf Coast. She's from California. Sometimes she said if she hadn't met Dad she'd still be living in Santa Monica.

A black labrador barked at them half a block away and a silky terrier started up about the same time. The lab could see them between the slats in its fence. The terrier sat in a window and waited for them. The lab snarled and lunged against the fence. Last year it knocked out a board but couldn't get its shoulders through the gap and sat inside with its head sticking out. For a while, I watched it from my window. I think it got bored with nothing exciting to see and eventually pulled its head back inside its fence. By the time the Bergmans got home from work, its head had disappeared. Mr. Bergman got his fence fixed that night and that was the last time the Lab pushed out a board on the fence.

The terrier never came outside unless the lady carried it and she never put it on the ground. She only brought it out that I could see when she went to the store. The dog sat in her lap as she drove or it stood to stare through the car window and she let it. It looked like an alien.

Our neighborhood was a small bunch of houses at the edge of a small bay town, a village set on top of a bluff looking west across bay water. Our neighborhood had four streets if the street bisected by the entrance road was counted as two.

Surrounding the cluster of our houses was what's left of some small farms with abandoned fields and pecan orchards, overgrown in tallow trees and briars and yaupon bushes. Rabbits lived in holes deep into the thickets and came out at night to eat the lawn grass. Feral cats stalked them and sometimes coyotes hunted them both. Roger stayed in at night. He slept in my oldest sister's room.

There was an empty lot across the street from my house. One of six left empty, owned by a man whose family used to own the hundred acres that was there before he sold it off in bits and snatches. What he had left were six lots. Three acres, he was holding to make some money on before he died. Dad made fun of him and called him Emperor Jones. Dad didn't like anybody with more money than him. Or more stuff than him.

On the empty lot in front of us, an oak tree filled its corner, a coastal live oak maybe a hundred years old, elephant large, trunks and limbs arched into a green vaulted dome before bending to earth. Standing under it was like being in a cathedral. The rest of the ground was scraped bare and growing field grass. The dirt itself was tight clay, old seabed holding kernels of ironstone sitting mixed in with sandstone-peas like bb's scattered on sandy patches of eroded clay where nothing could grow, not even weeds.

When Dad had our front yard landscaped, they told him the clay was filled with iron, "microscopic dust that settled on the ancient ocean floor and sometimes coalesced into nodules of black orbs, iron stone, pebbles of molecular attraction." Dad snorted after they left and said it sounded like so much bullshit to him that this ground ever sat at the bottom of any ocean.

In the summer when the man and his dog came down the street, he said he named her Liesl for the girl in Sound of Music, she would stop under the oak and lie down to watch whatever might be moving. The man told Dad one afternoon that Liesl was a sight hound, called a Tazi from Asia, an ancient Asian hound, that's why she watched everything. Sight hounds hunt by seeing what they're chasing to kill. Chase and kill, that's what the man said they did. Dad said the man was full of crap. They didn't have hounds in China. The Chinese raise dogs to eat. That's where the word chow comes from. He said it's just lazy. That's why it sits under the tree. With all that hair it was just a fashion statement.

Before Roger, I had a dog. It didn't have to go walking in the street. It lived in the backyard. It had a pen back there where it stayed. Dad got it from a woman in Tipton who had a bunch of puppies to get rid of. We didn't know what kind it was but Dad said it looked like it had lab in it and some other stuff, maybe pointer. It was ugly when it was grown. Once it snapped at Dad when he was whipping it for digging a hole by the house. Dad took it off somewhere. I think to the pound.

Dad couldn't use it for hunting 'cause it couldn't retrieve a stick. I think he really wanted a duck-hunting dog but he was hoping the free one would do. Dad was cheap like that. He worked with it in the back yard at night when it was a puppy trying to get it to fetch. Sometimes it did. Mostly it'd just get the stick and take it off in the yard to chew on it. Dad would end up getting mad at it, and then put it back in the pen where it'd sit and look at him while he cussed it. It took Dad a few minutes to wind down enough after that to come inside the house. Mom didn't let him talk like that inside. Even so, me and my sisters went to other rooms or out the front door when he came in 'cause none of us wanted to be around for about another hour. If he saw you, he'd ask what you were doing and then no matter what you said he'd ask you if you didn't have anything better to do. Even though he didn't go hunting much, I don't know why he didn't get a real hunting dog. The man used to say; "You can't get something for nothing."

I named that dog Smith. Dad said that was a strange name for a dog and when I asked him why; he said it didn't mean anything. He called it Nails. He told me that was a good dog name since it meant something. It meant the dog was tough. My dog wasn't tough though. He was a good dog.

Dad said anybody could see the man's fancy dog wasn't much. It wasn't any real hunting dog. It had long blond hair and skinny bones. Dad said that the man was more than likely not feeding it enough. "That's why it can't walk the whole way around the neighborhood without plopping down in the shade to rest." Dad said he wouldn't have any dog that wasn't tougher than that. Besides, he wouldn't be letting any dog of his do whatever the hell it wanted to do if he was out taking it on a walk. Not that he would be taking any dog for a walk. That would have been my job.

Dad got that way about things. Mom said it was why he made such a good salesman. He sold equipment to the ship builders across the bay and I think he made a lot of money. He never took no for an answer. She said that he kept at somebody until they gave up. That's why she ended up marrying him.

In the summer, the man and his dog would stop under the oak tree in the lot across the street from our house. Holding her head straight up while she lay under the cathedral oak, the dog looked like the Sphinx. She had a long neck and ears fell flat on her neck with long hair so she didn't look like she had dog ears, watching everything, holding her long nose down so you didn't see it and only her eyes staring at you when you're out in your yard. The man would stand by her holding the lead stretched out so it dangled loose and she could get up and run a few feet if she wanted to before he would start running behind her.

I asked him why he did that. He said he wanted her to enjoy being outside. He said that she was the one that wanted to see the neighborhood not him. When he stood by her, he stared at the clouds or into the arched branches in the oak tree while he talked to her like she understood him. I asked him what he was looking at in the clouds. He said he wasn't sure; shapes, maybe how they changed form as they moved across land while waiting for Liesl to decide she wanted to go somewhere else. Sometimes he would comb her hair if they stopped a long time. He did that until she stood, stretched out, and then they left, suddenly, running off in whatever direction she chose.

Except one day there was an explosion and white light and lightening struck the tree, split it down the center core and it flopped over in two halves, peeled apart splintered oak heart naked in the sun, and the man and his dog were laying out there too, with smoke curling up from them.

I looked up and saw a cloud shaped like a black and purple fist clinched across where the sun would have been with the rest of the sky blue in places and then the fisted cloud blew itself out into the Gulf where it dissipated before anyone else could come out and see it.

I ran across the street to see if they were ok but they weren't.

The man was burned in a streak down his chest. I could see the track of the bolt on his tee shirt, and his shoes were blown off his feet. He had some leather slip-ons he wore when he walked the dog in the street and no socks. The shoes were out in the lot and his feet, the soles of his feet, were burned black.

I didn't look long at his dog. I'd seen the wisps of smoke curling from her hair and that was enough. She had silky hair and the man was always combing it. In the sun, her hair glowed like platinum. He said he had a special set of brushes he used at his house to brush her that had brass pins to remove the static in her hair. If he didn't use the brushes he said her hair would float. And a chrome plated brass comb, he used that to brush her, too. That's what he used when they went out walking. I saw it in his hand, burned fingers around it. The smell and my thinking made me puke.

Mom came out running across the street and told me to go back to the house. I tried to tell her they were dead but she said to hush and she'd already called the ambulance. She said that was all anybody could do for them. I ran back to the house and watched them from our living room window.

After forever, the ambulance came and a fire truck and then two cop cars pulled in and parked over by the stop sign at the corner. Once they started arriving, it got crowded fast. The cops wandered around asking a few questions and writing in their little notepads and then another car showed up. It said coroner on the door and a woman wearing a grey suit got out and walked around the exploded tree while the ambulance men stood smoking cigarettes off to the side. The coroner woman talked to Mom a bit then leaned down to look at the dead man and his dog. She did that for a minute or two before she walked over to the ambulance men who started unrolling a black plastic bag between them.

That was about the time the dead man's wife came running down the street. She wasn't screaming or making any sound, just running hard so that you could hear the slap of her feet hitting the street on each step. The cops caught her before she got to the mess that was left of the man and his dog and then she dropped on her knees like there wasn't anything left that could hold her up. She wasn't a big woman but when she dropped, the cops couldn't seem to hold her from the ground. The earth was a magnet and she was a nail that got sucked into it and the cops struggled to hold her until they finally gave up and let her sit on the ground where she wrapped her arms around her head.

The sun was out after that cloud went out into the Gulf and it never rained, only that one blast of lightening, and that was it.

After an hour, the ambulance left with the dead man stuffed inside the plastic bag. They put the dog in a bag too, but the cops took it and the man's wife off somewhere, maybe to her house. The fire truck left before any of them since there was no burning wood or power lines down or anybody that needed rescuing. Then the coroner woman drove out with the ambulance. They were all gone and the only thing left of it all was splintered parts of live oak in the empty lot.

I wondered why God would kill him and the dog like that. I asked Dad about it when he got home from work and he said maybe he didn't like them. I asked Dad if he ever worried about God not liking him and he said no. When I asked him how he knew if God liked him he said, I ain't never been struck by lightening. Then he went in his bathroom and got a shower since it was late and almost time for supper.

When I went in the kitchen, I asked Mom why God didn't like the man and his dog and she wondered where I got the idea, so I told her what Dad said and she said that was nonsense and I should know better than believe it. God didn't kill people, but when I asked her who did, she said, nobody. It was just nature.

That didn't seem any better to me, maybe worse since you couldn't do anything about random. And if God didn't kill him then he didn't save him either, which made god random and church pointless.

On Wednesday night at prayer meeting, when they got to the part where you pray for sick, dead, and dying people I eased out of the pew and slipped outside to wait for it to be over. Mom didn't say anything and let me leave. After church, everyone stood around outside talking before going home and the preacher came up to me and asked if I was doing alright.

I told him, "Yes, sir," and let it go at that. He'd be praying for me if I said a man, dog, and oak got killed by nature in one blast of lightening so there wasn't any point in praying to god about anything, since, if god didn't kill them, god didn't stop them getting killed either. Which wasn't exactly the same as saying there wasn't any god, but it was close since it wasn't any kind of god the preacher believed in, and I figured the preacher wouldn't slow down enough to notice the difference. I didn't want him praying for me so I never said anything about praying or god to him or anybody else.

The preacher opened up his Bible. He looked down at me and said, Son, I want to read you some scripture before you go home tonight.

I hated him calling me son. He wasn't my dad, but since he was the preacher I had to stand there polite with mom and my sisters and listen. Standing out there on the front steps of the church under a porch light with the June bugs in the dark while he started reading the Bible at me.

"All flesh is not the same flesh; but there is one kind of flesh of men, another flesh of beasts, another of fishes, and another of birds."

I wasn't sure where he was headed with that one but I could tell Mom had already told him about the man and his dog getting killed.

"There is one glory of the sun, and another glory of the moon, and another glory of the

> stars; for one star differeth from another star
> in glory. So also is the resurrection of the
> dead. It is sown in corruption; it is raised in
> incorruption. It is sown in dishonor; it is
> raised in glory. It is sown in weakness; it is
> raised in power. It is sown a natural body; it
> is raised a spiritual body. There is a natural
> body, and there is a spiritual body."

He went on like that for another couple of minutes and finally got to the part where Paul told the Corinthians, "*O death, where is thy sting? O grave, where is thy victory?*" That part I remembered from my Grandpa's funeral.

But it didn't make me believe there was any reason for the man and his dog being killed, then or now. I had seen the black-cloud fist, what the preacher had not seen, and it wasn't Bible words. It was pointless. I told him, Yes, sir, and, after he patted me on the shoulder and shook mom's hand, we were able to go home. That was the last time I went on Wednesday night and later I quit going on Sunday too. Mom let me alone about it and Dad never went anyway so it was easier to quit than I had thought.

The oak stayed splintered and split like that for a month or more, changing from green to dead, leaves dropping like fish scales, not the golden brown of when they get shed but a gray dead clinging on the twigs and branches until something knocked them down or a wind tore them off.

I was looking out at the hulk of it the day the chainsaws came and chopped it up and the trucks hauled it away. They left oak chips and acorns scattered across the dead leaves. The stump was a jagged cut where they left it the way it split.

After the man and dog got killed, I was over by the oak tree looking at the place where they were laid out on the ground and I saw a silver shining in the leaves. When I leaned over and dug into the dead leaves, I saw it was the man's special comb. It must have come out of his hand when they put him in the bag. I held it in my hand, chrome blistered in places from the electric charge that tore through it. It was heavy. The dead man carried it with him every day to comb Liesl. He might have been combing her when they were killed. I got a cold shiver holding it after him.

I went home with the dead man's comb in my pocket and sat in my room with it, holding it to feel the weight of it. There were worn places on the teeth where the tarnished brass showed. I felt the worn places and they were smooth, polished by endless grooming. I ran my thumb over the blistered chrome bubbled by lightening like the man's skin was burned black. Dad said the man deserved to get blasted by lightning for standing under a tree. Just because his dog wanted to sit in the shade was no excuse to be stupid. Dad said the man should have made Liesl do what he wanted 'cause it was just a dog. That's the way Dad was. He had no imagination. He used to say a bird in the hand's worth two in the bush.

I put the dead man's comb back in my pocket and carried it with me everywhere after that.

I walk through neighborhoods and rest under trees like the man and his dog used to do and watch the clouds change from cotton beds to thunder fists as they move over land. You can't be afraid of random. Nobody lives forever anyway.

I don't have a dog yet but someday I will get one. A dog like Liesl, and I will comb her hair with the silver comb and we will walk through neighborhoods and rest under trees just like it ought to be.

Mr. Thompson and the Curse
of Magic House

Melissa Vicknair had an apartment in an old house near Geary, a classic San Francisco two story Victorian with upstairs bedrooms converted to rentals sometime in the last century. She found it at the start of her junior year in college and had lived there ever since. She had no desire to move. It was her magic place. The place where she changed from student to graduate, the place where, she once said, she unwrapped from her cocoon.

Arriving home from the airport on a Saturday afternoon, Melissa paused half way up the walk to the front steps so that she could admire the house with its turret and gables. It had character. Even in November light, it was obvious to her that the house was special in that row of Victorians. Melissa stepped up on the porch, unlocked the front door, and entered the house's foyer. The best part of being gone was coming back.

"M, is that you?" Allison was in the kitchen again. In Melissa's ears, that saccharin voice was fingernails on a chalkboard, sand inside tennis shoes. Allie had moved into the other upstairs apartment last year, moved over from the east bay, from Oakland or Berkeley. Melissa wasn't sure exactly where, just from over there. Allie liked making spaghetti sauces from scratch with hours of simmering in an iron pot that she said was her grandmother's. The house smelled of garlic and oregano.

"S'me." Melissa answered on her way up the stairs to her apartment. They were supposed to share the kitchen and rooms downstairs but Allie had consumed it with her spices and recipes and parties.

"How was the trip?" Allie called from the kitchen, happy, always happy. She was worse before throwing a party, chipper and smiling. She acted like Jesus Christ was coming to visit.

"Fine." Melissa didn't pause on the stairs. "But I'm exhausted. I'm just going to turn in early."

"I have some friends coming over later. That's not going to bother you is it?"

Melissa unlocked her door. "No, that's ok. I'll turn on some music or something."

She closed the door and dropped her bag onto the floor at the foot of the bed. The wood floor had its original dark chocolate stain, thick as paint, with traffic places worn smooth through, down to the golden grain. The dark floorboards heightened her sense of the room's distant ceiling. It seemed higher than it was, as much a canopy as anything, or an ancient sky with water stain clouds.

She turned on her desk lamp and sat by the window. A week of jets and cities across the southeast, Melissa had travel buzz shimmering under her skin. Tomorrow the buzz would fade and on Monday, she would be normal and back among the stacks of books at NeuFiels. End of vacation, end of writer tour. A cup of hot tea would be good.

In her room, Melissa had assembled a small kitchen of essential appliances, microwave, espresso maker, toaster oven, electric kettle, and mini refrigerator. In her room, she could cook anything she wanted, which was nice. Other than taking out the garbage and washing her dishes, there was no need for her to go downstairs to the main kitchen where Allie baked and chopped and stirred her concoctions.

Melissa filled her kettle with filtered water and switched it on; a nice chrome electric she bought at Williams-Sonoma over the summer.

The city chilled with wet air rolling in across the Pacific. Tea would be nice. When the water boiled, she slowly poured it over the China Black and set the timer for five minutes. Outside her window, a black cat landed on the windowsill, accurately timing its jump from the swaying limb of a birch tree. The cat arched its back and waited for her to open the window.

She had named the cat Mr. Thompson but never talked to it. An old woman who lived next door to her parents used to talk to her cats. Melissa told her parents that Mrs. Keller was crazy and now, not wanting to go down that road, she refused to talk to the cat. It wasn't hers anyway. She didn't know where it came from or where it went.

Melissa slid the window open and the cat sat balanced on the sill between inside and outside. It never stepped into the room, always ready to slip back into the dark as easily as it had appeared. She took a saucer of food from the refrigerator and placed it on the sill. The cat sniffed it but did not eat. It never ate. For years it had appeared, sat on the sill and then disappeared, never eating anything that she presented. She offered the food without expecting it to eat, raised the window without expecting it to enter, and it never did either. The cat only sat on the sill and watched her with almond amber eyes.

One day, years ago, after the first week of Mr. Thompson's visitations, Melissa did not offer food when it appeared. The cat sat on the sill and squalled at her until she took a can of kipper snacks from the cabinet, opened the lid, and placed them on a dish in front of it. Mr. Thompson inspected the offering, turned, and disappeared without eating. Since that time, Melissa kept a dish of food in the refrigerator ready to offer when the cat appeared.

Tonight Mr. Thompson sat on the sill and watched her sip hot tea and nibble shortbread cookies. When she prepared a second cup of tea, he yawned and cleaned a paw.

For no reason that she could later recall, Melissa leaned toward the window and whispered very softly to the cat, "There's going to be a party tonight. One of Allie's."

Mr. Thompson stopped cleaning its paw and looked in her face with its empty eyes.

"I don't like her." Melissa sipped her tea and nibbled a bit of cookie. "I wish she never moved in here. I wish things were the way they were before she came."

She said no more and stared into her cup at the specks of leaves drifting in the bottom. Mr. Thompson resumed licking its paws and, when she finished tea, it disappeared.

It wasn't long after Mr. Thompson left the window that the doorbell rang and she heard the first voices of loud strangers. And so it went for the next hour, intermittent doorbells and loud voices gathering beneath her feet until the constant sound of the gathered crowd seeped up through the floor, between the floor boards, up the stairs, and under her door, laughter and loud voices.

Melissa slipped into her yellow flannel pajamas and sat in her bed with her book, a book she'd bought at the Atlanta airport to kill time while waiting for a flight to Pensacola. It was a McMurtry book she'd bought on a whim. One of his cowboy books, a period piece not contemporary. Cowboys and Indians and prostitutes in Texas, not her usual fare but she believed she should stretch herself a bit. McMurtry was supposed to be good even though he was from Texas. It was a hole in her reading that made her feel uncomfortable. As if she had time to read every book in the world.

Downstairs, the doorbell rang and the noise of the gathering crowd began to match the chaos of the men in the book. They were difficult to ignore. She slipped out of bed and steeped another cup of tea. Night chill crept through the window glass. The hot tea warmed her while she sat in the chair by the window and listened to downstairs voices, specks of words that drifted up the stairs. Outside, the cat was gone. She didn't see him anywhere. That was the way he was. At least, she thought he was a he. She wondered where Mr. Thompson went when he left her.

The floorboards creaked outside her door and Allie shouted through it, "Come'on down, M. We're having a party."

"That's ok." Melissa drew her legs up and tucked her knees tight into her chest. "I'm a little tired tonight. Maybe another time."

Other voices outside her door, she wasn't sure how many, broke into a cacophony of "Come on, M. Come join the party." Ignoring them was impossible, so she got out of bed, pulled on her robe, and opened her door intending to make them stop.

"Surprise!" Alley and her friends stood arrayed about her door, holding wine glasses and bottles and platters of breads and cheeses. "I knew you wouldn't come downstairs." She told her friends, "M is such a recluse." She whirled back to Melissa, "So we brought the party up here to you!" and wedged past Melissa into the room, handing her a glass of Shiraz as she passed. "It's your welcome home party! M just got back from a tour of the south, you guys."

"Really," came voices of disinterest.

"She's a writer you know. Isn't that right, M."

The crowd moved into her room, found places to sit, her bed, her chair, windowsill, the floor.

"How many books have you written?" That came from a dark haired guy standing in the corner of her room. She thought of Rasputin.

A red headed girl, pale as milk, like Molly Ringwald in 16 Candles, shouted while she waved her arm in the air over the heads in front of her, "I wrote a book once."

"What is your book about?" A bald headed older man, manicured fingers, laser trimmed hair, slick like Dick Cheney holding a half empty glass in his hand, leaned too close to her, spectacled eyes sweeping from her around her room. "Is it a novel?"

"Here, M. Let me fill your glass." Allie emptied the last of a bottle of Shiraz.

Melissa looked around her room, filled with faces of people she did not know, and smiled at them as though she had invited them. It was the polite thing to do. That's what her mother taught her. Melissa told Allie, "Thanks for the wine."

"So, M, you want to do a reading for us? We're dying to hear what you wrote."

"I don't know, Allie. I'm exhausted."

"We won't leave until you do. Will we." Ally swept her hand toward her guests.

"No, oh no," they all said on cue.

"After all, you spent a whole week down there." Allie moved around the room with a tray of cheeses, offering them to each person.

"Yeah, down in the red states." Cheney refilled his wine glass and slipped a slice of Tilsiter into his mouth.

Rasputin reached across to pluck a slice of Dubliner from the tray. "Why did you go down there?"

"The deep south is like a whole different country." A tall man, Abraham Lincoln thin with pinched long face and straight jet black hair cut in jagged gashes propped himself in the corner by her microwave and made an hors d'oeuvre out of a square of toasted wheat bread, Brie, and caviar.

Molly found a spot to sit cross-legged, leaning against the closet door. "Did you see any rednecks?" Allie passed her a half empty bottle of Shafer Merlot.

"You guys. She's from the south." Allie passed a tray of breads to a knotted group of three clinging to the corner of the door, Harpo, Zeppo, and Groucho. They weren't funny as people, only talking among themselves.

"Really." Rasputin examined her through the clear bell of his wine glass.

Molly smiled with perfect teeth and asked, "Where are you from, M?"

"Louisiana."

"Are you a Cajun? You don't look like a Cajun." Cheney emptied his glass and passed it to Allie for a refill. She poured the end of the Louis Jadot into it. He told her, "That's a good Pinot Noir. A nice bouquet."

"No. I'm from the other side of the state. A town up the river from New Orleans named Dutch Bayou." Melissa opened her carry-on bag and took out a marked up copy of her novel. "I'll read a few pages from the opening." It was the only way to get rid of them.

She read them the set of pages that she had been reading in independent bookstores and to reading clubs across the south. The group in her room listened and when she finished they clapped and told her it was really quite good. "Oh, yes," they agreed among themselves.

"Your characters were quite realistic." Allie glanced around the room at her guest's glasses and plates. "Anyone want some more wine?"

Rasputin leaned toward Melissa, blocking the light from her desk lamp and casting a shadow against her wall. "How much of the story is true?"

"It's fiction," Melissa said.

"Yes, we know," Rasputin sighed. "But it seems so familiar."

"It's set in Istanbul," she said. "Would that be familiar to you?"

Rasputin challenged her, "The description of the estate is based on the tea garden in Golden Gate."

"That was Yildiz Park in Istanbul." She dared him to lie, "Have you been to Istanbul?"

He took a different critical tack, "It seems to me that San Francisco would have been a better setting."

She laughed at him but had thought the same thing herself several times during the tour so she said, "The protagonist was an archaeologist. She was investigating Roman ruins under the city."

He mumbled "I didn't get that part," ducked his head and she knew she had him if she wanted.

"It was just an excerpt." She smiled. "It would have been a different story if it was San Francisco."

Molly jumped into the exchange, "Your dialog is so realistic."

"Thank you," Melissa said and slipped her book back into her bag. The moment was gone.

"How many copies have you sold?" Cheney swirled the dregs of wine in his glass.

"I don't know, yet. It just came out last month."

Allie leaped to her feet shouting to everyone that they shouldn't move, that she'd be right back. The room hushed and all eyes watched her sprint to the door, her bare feet with burgundy painted toe nails flashing across the floor boards, running down the hall to her apartment. Quickly she was back, dragging a large flat shipping box.

"I forgot to tell you. This arrived yesterday. It's from someplace in Alabama."

"My painting." Melissa took the box from Allie. "I bought a painting last week."

Molly moved to stand beside the box. "It's so large."

Abe looked up from placing a second wedge of Camembert on his platter. "What is it?"

"Where are you going to hang it?" Allie steadied the box while Melissa tried to pull the strapping tape off.

Harpo left the corner of her door to crowd in with the others around the box, "Quick open it. We want to see." Groucho and Zeppo watched without moving closer.

Melissa took a paring knife from her desk and slit the tape holding the box together. The cardboard side dropped and revealed a painting hiding underneath an inch of bubble wrap. A painting of a pasture and an oak tree with three cows standing under it.

Cheney joined the group around the painting, "Why did you buy that?" He stood with an empty wine glass, looking down his nose at Harpo.

"It's big." Harpo edged away from Cheney. "What is it?"

Melissa peeled off the bubble wrap and leaned the painting against her headboard so that all of them could see it. "It's a primitive perspective."

The group stared at the painting while sipping wine and nibbling cheese and bread.

"Perspective," repeated a longhaired brunette looking like Terri Hatcher in Lois and Clark.

Allie said, "I don't get it," and conversations erupted around the room about the meaning of perspective and the symbolic use of cows in the composition.

"Three cows. Three is a holy number," said Terri.

"But why cows," Allie protested. "Why not some other animal. Something like cats.

They're very Egyptian. But cows? God. That's so rural."

And after that, conversations raged around the bedroom about the meaning of cows, why not cats or horses, and what did the Egyptians have to do with it anyway.

Terri reminded them that Hindus believed cows were sacred.

"But this is from Alabama." Abe sat on the floor in front of the closet. "I don't think they have Hindus or Buddists in Alabama. My god that's in the middle of the south."

Rasputin said, "It could be a sexist statement about women in society."

Terri and Molly booed him while the room erupted in laughter.

Allie tilted her head so that her hair draped across her face and her eyes focused on Melissa, "I still don't know why you would buy something like this."

Melissa leaned against the wall by her bed and studied the painting, the out of perspective fence and 2-dimensional cows arranged under an oak tree in a field. "I like it."

'It's so bourgeois." Allie's voice went up a shrill octave. On the sound of the word bourgeois, the room went cold. "You're not actually going to hang it in here are you?"

Melissa decided to obfuscate, "Do you mean Bourgeois the artist? Or are you talking about the piece itself?"

Allie waved her arms in the direction of the painting, "The piece. It's cows in a pasture for christ-sake."

Melissa frowned at her. "It's primitive art, actually. Not bourgeois. That would be something you'd buy at the furniture store to hang over your dining table or couch. I suppose even a Pollock could become bourgeois if society changed to encompass it." This set off a round of small conversations about the meaning of art in society.

Allie whispered furiously to Abe, "It doesn't match my décor." She whispered to Cheney, "It's the sort of painting a farmer would want."

In her usual style, instead of defining the line between them with an, "It's my apartment not yours," Melissa blinked and out of her mouth came, "Farmers are not members of the bourgeoisie. Except for mega farmers. They might be." She trailed off, lost in mental tracking, tracing differences between a farmer that was working a hundred acres in Louisiana and a Midwest or California farmer with fields that reached beyond sight. She'd seen the spread of fresh plowed rows on rows outside Salinas, reaching from the 101 back across the flat to the steep hills and wondered in that moment how her cousin, Bobby Perrilloux working his place in Gramercy could keep up with commercial farms like that. Bobby wouldn't have wanted a painting of three cows. If he wanted any painting at all it would be his bird dog or bass boat.

Around the room, conversations shifted in weird ways from cows, cats, and art to politics, sex, and the price of gasoline. Abe was talking with Allie about the Brie de Maux, where did she find it, and Allie told him she had made a trip over to the Cheese Board in Berkeley. She said she used to live near there, before she moved into the city. She still made weekly trips to shop for her favorites.

Melissa stood in the midst of voices holding her half empty glass cursing her mother who raised her to Be sweet, Be nice, Share. She tapped the glass rim against her front teeth, tapping out her frustration. Allie was ooze, a fungus spreading through the house, too pleasant to suspect until her décor was everywhere infecting the house with superficial intellect. And Melissa was what Mother taught her, smiling, retreating, and waiting for that transcendent moment that never came when Karma would restore balance to the house.

Allie shouted, "Guys, we should go downstairs. I have to check on the sauce and put the bread in the oven." As she passed through the door she added, "And I have a new Coltrane CD I want you to hear."

Her group followed en mass.

Harpo told Melissa, "Congratulations on the new book," as he left the room.

Rasputin, the last to leave, asked her if she wanted him to close the door.

"Sure," she said and he pulled it softly closed behind him.

Melissa leaned back on her bed to stare at the water stain clouds across her ceiling, sipped wine from her glass, and listened to the piano and sax downstairs mix into the laughter of voices and the clatter of plates and pots and pans. She closed her eyes but would not sleep.

She had three choices, move out, fight, or kill Allie, and smiled that killing Allie was an option. Of course, she would not. However, she could always mix arsenic into

Allie's spices, and she wondered how much it would take and where she could get it. She wasn't a mystery writer and didn't know such things. Maybe she should change genres.

She drank the last of her wine.

At the sound of a tap against the window glass, her eyes opened and saw Mr. Thompson on the sill. "I see you," she murmured and crossed the room to open the window. The cat stepped inside onto her table and sat, looking at her with iridescent eyes.

"No more food tonight," she told it but the cat wasn't hungry and made no sound but sat on the table by the window watching her. Melissa placed her empty wine glass on the table and sat in the chair by the cat. She picked up the McMurtry book intending to read while she waited for the cat to want to leave.

As she turned pages to find her place, she told Mr. Thompson that there really was no karma, redemption, or salvation. "Priests invented it to make people happy."

The cat said nothing.

Of course, she wasn't serious about killing Allie. That's what she told the cat. It was a fantasy. She just wanted Allie gone.

She told the cat that tomorrow she would go downstairs and move Allie's dishes out of her share of cabinets in the kitchen and she would fix her toast downstairs in her toaster and buy groceries to fill her half of the refrigerator.

The cat stared at her with its hollow eyes.

She looked up from the print in the paperback and whispered to the cat that next weekend she was going to have a party and invite everyone from the bookstore to fill the living room and they would play classic Zeppelin and King Crimson, but no jazz. Allie liked jazz. Just metal. Maybe some Slayer, even if Allie didn't like it.

Mr. Thompson softly slipped back into the black.

Melissa leaned over, closed the window behind him, and turned out her light. She decided that Mr. Thompson was actually cursed by a witch or magi in another life, perhaps for an evil deed or an act of cowardice, and, transformed, must sit by day as a pharonic statue at the front door unseen in the shadows of the holly shrub and watch over the house for eternity. On occasion when the curse permitted him to come to life, he could visit its occupants, sit on her windowsill and watch life but not eat.

Tomorrow. She decided to try and find him tomorow. Then, smiling with the image of Mr. Thompson sitting in the dark at the front door guarding the house, she slept.

Downstairs the front door opened and closed and the crowd noise ended and it was silent again in the house on a street near Geary.

- Cocobolo -

The Insanity of
Winston

I

Winston was high strung. Everyone that knew him said so to each other. His mother would tell the story every year at Thanksgiving of the time when he was in high school and decided to create a habitat for nesting bluebirds. Each year when she began with "let me tell you about the time," Winston would smile politely at his relatives and then ease his way from the room. Strangely, his mother believed the story made him sound noble or charming. He attempted to be out of the room by the time that she began telling how he took a compass and tape measure to calculate the optimum height and direction for the bluebird box to face. At that point his mother was caught up in her own remembrance and would not notice Winston's absence.

Winston calculated that the box had to face east toward the house and the opening had to be 5 feet from the ground. His father told him he'd just nail the damn thing up there and be done with it but not Winston. He had to measure it all out. So he was out there in the winter putting up that box. In the spring when a pair of bluebirds arrived and made their nest in the box, she told everyone, he was so excited. He set up his father's spotter scope on a tripod in the den and watched the birds flying in and out of the yard. Every morning he was up at dawn to record their activities. He had a small journal in which he kept his notes.

Winston would go into the kitchen while she told the same story each year and eat a second slice of pie. Lemon meringue was his favorite because it was what his grandmother brought each year when he was a child. She was dead by the time of the telling of the bluebird story. His mother tried to make it for him but her recipe was not the same. It was a gelatin-based pie not custard but he ate it anyway while thinking of his grandmother and wishing she had told them how to make the pie.

Soon there would be laughter when his mother got to the part about him trying to keep the mockingbirds away. After the laughter they would be silent when she told them about him finding the dead female bluebird under the oak tree and his opening the box to discover the dead babies. The male bluebird flew up to the box several times after that but eventually he stopped returning. Winston said he hated mockingbirds after that. Said they drove the female into the ground while she was returning to the box one evening and killed her.

There wasn't much left to the story after that. Except the part about his shooting the mockingbirds, which his mother always left out, and his taking down the box and burning it on a cinder block in the back yard, which she did tell but so sadly, someone would have to change the subject before Thanksgiving was ruined. His dad would usually tell the story about the dog falling into the pool. It didn't matter what story as long as it was funny.

She did that every year until he was out of college and moved to Los Angeles. From that point on he never went back for Thanksgiving. For all he knew she was still telling the same story each year.

In Los Angeles, Winston had a girlfriend. He loved her and after several months he suggested they rent a place up in the hills. Winston was working in Culver City for a studio and his new girlfriend worked in a café in West Hollywood serving sandwiches and lattes. She was in a couple of episodes of a TV series on cable but hoped to get a bigger gig on a network show or a movie of the week. Eventually she was going to make the connection. Someone eating lunch at the café would be the break. That's what she believed. That's all she needed. She told Winston that once or twice a week. Winston got tired of telling her it was never going to happen and that year went quickly past and nothing happened.

Winston was an accountant working for a studio and Zizzie, his girlfriend, believed that he was going to help her make her break. But the accounting building was not on the studio lot. It was in an office building like any other building. He brought home the newsletters from work with the studio logo and bits of news about events in the lot and she read each one for clues to the inside track. They attended department picnics and company parties at which Zizzie moved through the crowd looking for faces of actors she had brushed against when working the TV episodes or faces she had seen. Generally the crowd was finance or back office production crew and they would leave each party with Zizzie glum and staring out of the car at Los Angeles as they went back up the hill to the house that was in a canyon and around a bend.

Winston loved the houses, arranged in layers, stacked against the hill, with spindly stilts supporting their floors in space. There was no yard to mow. Except in winter, there was no rain to make grass grow. There was only the house hanging in air above the canyon and a deck open to the weather. He would stand out on the deck; glass doors open behind him so that the inside was not separate from the outside. He would stand on the deck without walls behind him and stare at the green shades across space where the other canyon wall rose, broken in intervals by corresponding layers of balconies and decks wrapped around the outer edges of other houses. He would stand on the deck and wish he could own the house. He would wish that he would not have to move when the lease ended and the owner moved back from Europe. He would stand on the deck and try to compute a solution that would allow him to remain while Zizzie slept on the sofa in the space behind him. Those were the good days. On the bad days the air was grey and orange from fumes collected in the basin and stagnant, rising up the canon walls, filling it with murk until he could not see the green across space and he wondered why he lived in that place. On those days he closed the glass doors and stood inside looking out at fog of diesel smoke and gasoline exhaust and wonder what it looked like before Americans arrived. On those days Zizzie would cough and not sleep and Winston would watch her reflection in the door glass as she sipped Pinot Noir from a bell shaped wine glass and ate smoky gouda on cracked pepper crackers.

At night he would drive Zizzie down the canyon to Santa Monica where they would eat and walk the pedestrian mall. He was a tourist and she was his guide. Each Saturday morning they drove up PCH through Malibu until they reached Ventura and then would turn around and drive back. Late lunch was at Geoffry's Malibu. A Spicy Shrimp Salad for Winston with Herb Crusted Salmon for the entrée. He ordered that every Saturday. Zizzie never ordered the same thing. She had no favorites and teased him at first for never trying anything else. Eventually she stopped.

They sat at tables outside under the umbrellas and watched the boats in the cove and the ocean beyond. Winston looked for seals and dolphins. Zizzie complained about the wind even behind the glass walls that blocked it. Winston argued at first but ignored her later. The sound of the surf dulled the sound of her complaints and later she became quiet when he bought her a Resolution jacket from Roxy. She wore that when they made their Saturday drive on PCH.

On the first trip up PCH, Zizzie told him let's stop at Geoffrey's. She said it used to be Holiday House. Had he ever heard of Holiday House? He hadn't and she figured as much. She told him that it was built in the glory days after the end of the second war and everybody in Hollywood went to Holiday House. Even JFK and Marilyn Monroe, that's where they had their rendezvous. He was a senator when that happened. And Frank Sinatra, everybody went to the Holiday House. Now it was Geoffrey's. Can't you just imagine, she would say when they were sitting at a table with their drinks, seeing Lana Turner at a table over there with Rita Hayworth over there or maybe Frank Sinatra.

Winston said he couldn't and would sip his wine and glance around the room to see if there was anyone in it that he might recognize from TV. He was certain he wouldn't recognize them even if they were there.

Winston wondered what Malibu looked like when it was a retreat from L.A. If he could make the drive each day he'd live there, if he could afford it. He asked Zizzie what people did for a living that lived there. She had no idea.

Zizzie had straight black hair cut like Cleopatra, or Elizabeth Taylor as Cleopatra. She looked like she belonged in Geoffrey's. That's what he told her and she glowed.

On Sundays they did nothing.

Winston loathed Sundays. Loathed because it was a dead day, too late to do anything before Monday, not long enough to begin anything, the day he returned home if he was away. It was suspense without reward. Watching football in the winter and it was dark before the last game. A lost day, each week he sunk into a minor depression unless something tricked him into being happy. On Sunday morning he and Zizzie brunched at a café at the foot of the canyon, omelets, eggs Hollandaise, and Mimosas. Until midday he could shut out the blah of impending Monday with brunch. Once they were back up the hill though he would sit and watch the sun arc behind the canyon ridge and shade from the ridge reach out dark fingers to envelop the house.

One Sunday afternoon he stood and told Zizzie they should go for a drive. She asked him where but he hadn't decided and told her Las Vegas. They could be there by 8. She clapped her hands and laughed a high-pitched laugh and said that she didn't have anything to wear.

I don't care he told her. Let's just get the hell out of here. I don't want to see the sun disappear today. He walked to the door, snagging his car keys from the table in the front halls as he passed and Zizzie jumped over the back of the sofa to follow. In the car, he paused for her to slip inside before turning the key. The needle on the tach bounced before he backed into the street and was gone down the canyon road to the streets that lead him to the freeway. Zizzie sat beside him with her hair rippling in the wind.

When he got the job in Culver City he bought a used Boxster S. A silver convertible, he drove it to work every day. Sitting in the line of cars on the 101 made the idea of it ridiculous, inching forward until the breaks came in the line and everyone raced to hold their places while laggards dropped behind as cars jumped into spaces they could not defend. Hammering the brakes when the traffic slowed to nothing. It was no life for a Porsche - or any car. They should be riding motorcycles, motor scooters; all of L.A. should be buzzing around on Vespas. Vespas with men in suits and women in office costumes perched on their narrow seats. He laughed.

Driving the Boxster to Las Vegas was good. Sunday night traffic was coming back into L.A. not going out. At dusk the string of headlights and taillights in front of him traced a rosary across the desert. A rosary of gems, pearls, diamonds, rubies, and amethysts. Zizzie talked about people at work or people that came into the café who worked for studios and he agreed with her at odd times to keep her company but had no recollection later of what she said. She gave him hell when they got there and he turned around and drove back to L.A. He had to be at work in the morning and couldn't figure how she calculated they could do anything else. She was silent until the thermometer at Baker. She told him, it was the world's tallest thermometer, and by Barstow had somehow curled into the seat and was asleep.

He pulled into the driveway at 2AM and carried Zizzie inside. She weighed as much as a goose feather and wrapped her arms tight around his neck, which made it easy to negotiate the front door. Monday morning already.

Do you love me?

Zizzie was dressing for work when she asked him.

Of course I do. Winston was drinking coffee and reading the morning paper in the kitchen. He didn't have much time before he had to leave for work so he was mainly scanning headlines and intro paragraphs for anything interesting. Do you love me?

Silly. She wiggled into her jeans and was headed into the kitchen for her bagel and cream cheese.

Do you?

Naturally. She spread the cream cheese and took a bite. Have to go, she kissed him on the lips leaving him the taste of strawberry cream cheese and she was gone. He heard her Volvo crank. She needed to take it in for a tune-up. It was an old 760 wagon and needed regular oil changes and fresh plugs. She ignored it like all mechanical things. When it broke she would complain and buy something else that was old and cheap.

Winston folded the paper and placed it on the table. There was an interesting article about the evidence of geological subsidence in the Pacific Northwest but he didn't have time to read it. He would finish it after work. An hour to Culver City and an hour and a half home, it wasn't a symmetrical drive in terms of time. He wasn't sure why that was. At night on the return he tried to identify the causes for the extra time. The reasons changed each day but the length of time remained the same. The only variable might be additional accidents but the return transit time only lengthened never shortened.

Most of the people in his department lived in the beach communities. Manhattan Beach was one of the popular spots. One weekend when Zizzie was working, he went over to a party at a guy's apartment in Manhattan Beach. He had a hard time finding parking. There was never enough parking in L.A. but the streets were narrow and he didn't want any scratches on the Boxster so he was looking for something with some space around it. He ended up in a parking garage a couple of miles from the apartment and had to walk. The walk wasn't bad and he wasn't too worried about getting mugged but it gave him time to see the place and he decided it wasn't for him. There were no real trees or yards. The beach was close but he preferred the hills. Besides that, Zizzie would never leave the studio area. And she had her job at the café.

If he lived in Manhattan Beach though he'd knock an hour a day off of his commute time. That was 5 hours a week. Not to mention the cost of gas and maintenance on the Boxster. It added up. But he would never move.

He took the off ramp and left the freeway, driving north to the studio complex. He'd be there in the parking lot in 30 minutes.

On the drive home, Zizzie called and said she was covering the evening shift for Melissa who had called in sick. At a party more likely, but Jones had asked her to take the turn so they wouldn't be shorthanded during the after-theatre rush. She'd agreed and would be home late.

Winston said no problem and asked if she wanted him to fix her something but she told him no. She'd eat at the café before she left.

Winston asked her what time she thought she'd be in and she told him probably after 8. That's 12 hours he said and she'd told him it was ok. Jones was paying her OT so she didn't mind.

Al'right, if you say so. Winston couldn't think of anything else that he could say, told her he'd see her when she got in, and pressed the button to kill the call. It didn't happen very often, that she had to work late or fill in for someone else, but it annoyed him even though it wouldn't change much in his evening. She didn't cook. But it annoyed him anyway. He wondered why and puzzled along several lines of thought to isolate the reason. There was none, nothing rational.

Before driving up the canyon he stopped at Bar Marmont. Zizzie hated the place so they never went together. It would have been the sort of place he expected her to claim as a favorite but she denied it. Said it was for tourists, which was absurd since the entire city was a fabrication for tourists, but she refused to go. Parking was hell, but on nights when he was alone that's where he went. The crowd and noise filled space but inside the tall ceilinged rooms there was no sense of smallness. Winston would argue with Zizzie at first that the hotel and its bar were the core expression of life in L.A. In the Marmont there was no tomorrow. He wondered if Belushi liked the bar or did he just stay in the bungalow. She would leave the room and after a time he no longer mentioned the Marmont to her.

When he ate there, he would order a Diablo and a plate of grilled rosemary prawns. By the time the drink arrived he would order a second, which generally reached him as they landed the plate of prawns in front of him. Between the two drinks and the prawns he was satisfied until late night when Zizzie came home. She would bring a box of sandwiches and chips from the cafe. By that time he would be ready to eat again. She would expect him to eat and they would sit in front of the TV and watch Letterman or something recorded. Maybe one of the Harry Potters except that Zizzie was sick of those by now. It had become his compulsion to sit late at night and run them.

Zizzie always brought something from the café, even when she didn't work late. She didn't cook. For his mother cooking was a rite. For Zizzie it was oppression, something she shifted to someone else. At parties she would say that she cooked but he could count the meals she'd prepared that month on two hands. His mother wouldn't like her but would never say so. His mother was like that. But Winston would never take Zizzie to St. Helena. Zizzie was not interested in going. Life beyond the L.A. basin was pale to her. He wasn't sure anymore if she was wrong.

The valet brought his car around and Winston slipped him a 5. It was 30 minutes to the house. There would be time to watch a Harry Potter before Zizzie made it home. He continued down Sunset to his turn and drove up the canyon road.

Winston woke about 2AM with the TV still on and was confused. He was lying on the sofa. It wasn't Saturday night. He counted down the days and hadn't missed any. He turned off the TV and went down the hall to the bedroom and saw her lump under the covers in the bed. Zizzie hadn't wakened him when she came in. Quietly he took off his clothes, got his shower, brushed his teeth, and slipped under the covers next to her. Eased his arm around her naked waist. Her skin was hot to his and soft. After all, it wasn't important that she didn't like to cook.

II

Zizzie said she didn't want to drive up PCH. That was on a Saturday morning late in September. Winston had picked up his keys and was ready to leave while Zizzie was sipping her coffee and scrolling through the channel guide. She told him she was looking for a cooking show that used to run on PBS.

Why? He slammed the keys on the countertop. She flashed a glance at him before she picked a channel. It was a Julia Child. I remember this one from when I was a kid, she said.

We go up the PCH every Saturday.

It's boring. I want to do something different for a change.

When did you decide this? You didn't say anything about it before.

I just decided. Just now.

Winston sat at the table by the glass doors and looked across the canyon. His brain was already into the trip and dislocated. Options, he could drive up alone but risk pissing off Zizzie. He could stay and risk pissing off Zizzie who would say he was codependent, couldn't he do anything on his own. Why did she always have to be with him? She needed some space. Those were things she'd said before. *Lady or the Tiger.* Tiger. He picked up his keys. There was no smog yet and the morning sun hit the window glass across the canyon in gold sheets. Half of the fun on the drive was having her along. She didn't want to go. Why was that? Mac, his dad's friend, used to tell him, "Study long study wrong." Winston would say that was in golf. Mac said golf was an analogy for life. He had to get going or spend Saturday watching TV.

Where are you going?

I'm going to do the drive.

Without me?

I don't want to watch TV all day.

Do something around here. She waved her hand across the view from the deck.

I like driving up the coast.

Fine. She turned up the volume on the TV. Bon Appetite.

Zizzie was not happy but he was committed. He sat in the car with the engine running rethinking his options but decided there were none. Winston slipped into first and, top down, pulled out into the street. The Boxster needed the drive.

At Topanga Canyon, Winston took a left off of the PCH and rode up the twisty bits, holding the Boxster in third and downshifting to second until the apex of the corners, wanting to accelerate harder than the traffic permitted but didn't. The canyon was settled with houses back from the road, partially masked by oaks and occasional eucalyptus, clusters of small buildings, grocery stores, boutiques, cafes, and homes. The road climbed up the canyon, twisting back and forth, and the Boxster growled for him to turn it loose. Winston had considered taking the road on other Saturdays but with Zizzie along had passed it. She was along for the brunch in Malibu. He snapped glances at the places around him, recalled a bit of trivia about Sharon Tate being murdered somewhere around there and wondered where that had been. He didn't remember any details. Didn't know if the house was still there. Winston suspected that it had been torn down, replaced by another. That was how it was in L.A. History was short.

He drove smoothly, settling in the rhythm of the curves of the road, swinging into each bend. Traffic up Topanga was thin. The Boxster was happy. Morning light was bright and the shadows under the oaks by the road were made darker by it. In the corners when he cleared the canopy of oaks the sun blinded him with white light and he squinted until driving back under the shade of the oak canopy. Other than that the drive was ok.

His dad would have liked the oaks. The old man was a freak about trees. Didn't want them cut or removed. Every spring the neighbors would saw off the tops of their crepe myrtles and the old man would go ballistic. His mother would tell him to settle down before they heard him but it never slowed the old man down. Every year it was the same. The old man would ask all of them if they knew what arborists called it, cutting back crepe myrtles like that. He would tell them, they called it crepe murder, without waiting for an answer. Why the hell would anybody butcher a living organism like that? Criminal. As bad as maiming an animal. They'd put you in jail for doing that to a dog.

And the old man would run on like that for a few days. Said he was going to go over there one day and dig them up and plant them in his yard. One year he bought three from the nursery and planted them next to the neighbor's yard. He made certain they were the tallest growing crepe myrtles he could find and then he let them go, never cut them. After five years they were 20 feet and in ten they were over thirty. The neighbors ignored him. Eventually each spring their crepe myrtles would send out whip thin streamers of shoots in masses from the ends of their four-foot high stumps and in a few months after that there would be masses of blooms and the old man would grumble about how ugly they were. All color, no shape, no character and for a week he would rage in the living room whenever he walked by the front window and saw them. Winston's dad hated the neighbors because of that.

His dad would have liked the drive up Topanga. Would have liked it better before the Americans arrived. That's what his dad always said when they were watching TV and it was some show about something in California. I wonder what it looked like before the Americans arrived. The other thing his dad always said was, they filmed that in California.

Winston wondered why his dad settled back into St. Helena after he got out of the Army, didn't go back to California, instead he got married, had kids, the usual. Never left or lived anywhere else after that. He never said much about that. He wasn't the kind you wanted to ask either. Winston downshifted into second and accelerated through a left hand curve. The Boxster settled into the corner without sway and climbed into the straight.

Topanga was a good change from the usual L.A. chaos. Ten minutes of flickering between shade and sun before the trees beside the road turned to scrub and the grass on the hillside was broom straw with prickly pear cactus sprouting in clumps from gravel rock and flinty ground. The transition was a hard line of green treetops below dry grass and then there was the crest of the hill, broken off in front of him, a jagged line chipped in rock like the edge of an arrowhead he'd found in a field by his grandfather's house. In the cleft of the canyon where it rose to meet the ridgeline was the switch back in the road that took him over the top and he was across and into the valley beyond. There was no transition to city. It was a sudden arrival. Cut off by the ridgeline from Pacific wind, heat rose in thermal waves from the valley shimmering the air like water. The orange haze of car exhaust and blowing dust had not formed yet. That would be later, starting at the freeway and spreading across the valley floor, collecting in the bowl like nasty water. To him it wasn't a valley. It was a flat 10-mile wide land connection between ridges.

Winston drove to the Ventura Freeway. It was the only thing he could think of to do. He took the ramp back to L.A. Almost 11AM. That was too quick. He wasn't sure how he would explain it to Zizzie. Maybe he would say that the drive wasn't as interesting without her. She might like that.

She was sitting on the deck drinking an iced coffee and reading when he opened the door. She glanced at him but didn't seem surprised and said nothing. Winston stood in the living room confused since the scene hadn't gone as expected. The part where he had to admit it wasn't interesting without her had not happened and the house was silent. When he tossed his keys on the counter, the clunk of metal and plastic on granite were the only sounds in the place.

- Cocobolo -

Gravity

I can remember being in love if I think about it.

Sometimes I go back to the old places and I expect them to look the same as they did but they don't. I notice details I don't remember, raw brick walls and wobbly bistro tables, wooden chairs with missing back slats, unbleached paper napkins, concrete floors, and chipped linoleum.

Looking at it now, I guess the old coffee house is a dive.

On Friday evenings after work, I come back for a double espresso and sit at that table by the front window.

We used to sit there and watch people walk by and make up stories about them. I did and she listened.

I thought she was listening.

I would get a double shot and she would have a latte with caramel. Then she sprinkled cinnamon on top. I never said anything about the caramel or cinnamon but wondered why she would do that to good coffee. I never understood why she did that.

There's a lot that I don't understand.

I say that a couple times a day now. If she knew, she would say I've grown. What a crock. I'm screwed up. That's all.

Last week I read an article on the Internet about a scientist trying to design an experiment that would detect gravity leaking in and out of our existence. The idea, as I understand it, is that gravity is another dimension, one of the 10 or 12. I don't remember how many there are. And gravity particles might move between the other dimensions. There might be micro black holes that appear and disappear. It's all part of a physics thing called super string where every thing is really only a set of differently vibrating strings. What we see in the dimensions that we can comprehend are the representations of them.

I guess that makes us metaphors. Maybe love is one of those dimensions. Maybe it leaks in and out like gravity, a black hole that suddenly opens inside your chest and sucks all of your life inside it. Then it closes as quickly and we wander around lost in places where we were when it happened. And we don't understand what thing went wrong.

If gravity can leak then time should too I would think. This would explain why sometimes it skips and stops.

I remember sitting here one time when I was in love and time disappeared.

I reached out one morning to hold her hand and then it was afternoon. I remember wishing I could stay with her forever.

On Friday evening after coffee, I park under the pepper trees across the street from our house. Our house is a pale yellow now but back then, it was brown. The new owner repainted it. The trees have grown taller.

I don't like the way they trim the boxwood. They cut them back after they bought the house and began making the boxwood into a hedge. I had trimmed them in a bonsai slanting style. They looked interesting. Now they're just green boxes like everyone else's.

Out front on the sidewalk over there is where she told me she was moving out. Friday morning in October, we were leaving for work and she said, "We need to talk." My gut shriveled. I wanted to puke. I asked her when she wanted to talk and she said "after work."

Time stopped.

All day I waited for it.

I wonder if existence is more than what we know. I suspect that if I could see all 12 dimensions I would discover my real existence was different from the one that I thought I was living.

I always listen to Billie Holliday when I go over to the house even though I have a Frank Sinatra CD I bought this year. He sings about love, but from what I heard, he seemed to come out ok when love went bad on him. After all, he was Frank Sinatra. Billie gets closer to it for me.

On Friday nights after work, we would ride over to Mama Italia's and pick up a carryout tub of spaghetti and meatballs with garlic bread. We ate Mama's spaghetti for supper and watched old movies on Friday nights. It was our thing.

In October after the heat, she told me she was leaving. She said I yelled at her when she made mistakes, creased the car that time, that I was angry when I drove in L.A. traffic. Being near me made her sick to her stomach.

She told me she had decided to get an apartment over in Burbank, alone.

I sat on the curb. I held the pan of Mama's spaghetti on my knees while she talked. The dusk air was cool and the dark was beginning to squeeze between the lights across the valley.

I heard her say living with me made her feel like a prostitute. She hated the touch of my skin on her, lips, hands, fingertips. She said that. Keep the house. She didn't want anything of mine or from me, anything that was "we". Except Smokey our cat, she wanted him but she didn't want any of the fish or the aquarium. She said they were too much trouble and she never liked them anyway. They had been my idea. While she was still young, she wanted her own life again.

After the sun collapsed into the Pacific, everything was in view and a high-speed tremor ripped inside me. I watched my fingertips expecting them to dissolve in flurries of gold light, the atoms letting go of each other as the electron shells disintegrated. I wanted to collapse into the black hole that opened in my chest. I did not.

"A prostitute", I sat there. What could I say after that when the world was inside out? I let the spaghetti pan burn my knees. That was real. I held onto it.

October was a bad month. We lived in the house without anything to discuss. She never said anything about her lover but I felt someone in my shoes… a curious thing to say about sex. She would not tell me until Thanksgiving when we were locking the house and said she did not want to tell me about David because she was afraid that I might get mad and kill them. But I had surprised her about it all and now she thought it was ok for me to know.

Sometimes I wonder what in the hell goes on in her head. I wouldn't have done anything like that.

Later I might have dreamed about hunting him down and killing him with a double-barreled shotgun blast when he opened his front door, but not that first night and not her. Not sitting on the curb with lightening ripping my chest apart while she said she could not stand the touch of me and the air around her turned ice to me.

I gave the fish to the kid next door but they died. His parents wouldn't buy them filtered water.

It's time to head over to my room. I don't park by my house long on Friday night. I don't want to worry my old neighbors, so after a few minutes, I crank it up and drive to Studio City. When I get to the new place, I throw a frozen pizza in the oven.

I have a little convection oven that does a great job on frozen pizza. The fan fills the room with pizza smell. While the pizza is cooking, I turn on the science fiction channel and pour a finger of Glenlivet.

I keep four crystal glasses on my bookshelf but I use the same one every Friday night. The other three remain upturned. Maybe someday I might have company over. You never know.

She liked to say that I had no friends. A little, satisfied smile creeping from the corners of her mouth and that was when I thought we were in love, so God knows what it would be like now.

I pretended I didn't care. I had friends. I just didn't invite them over to the house, that's all.

While the pizza bakes, I sit in the room and watch sci-fi and drink scotch and life seems ok. After thirty minutes, the bell on the oven rings and the room smells like home. That's not a bad Friday night.

I don't drink the 'livet with my pizza. I like Margareta pizza and the combination of garlic and tomato doesn't fit with good scotch. I have a jug of red Rossi for the pizza.

We had a nice place in L.A. Up in the hills. Not too big and the view was great. In the fall, we could see the Channel Islands from up there. October used to be good. The Santa Anna's would come in off the mountains and break up the summer air.

Every year I used to look forward to October.

Tonight on the scifi channel, it's reruns of Stargate. The episode when alien bugs started eating humans. After sci-fi and pizza, I pour another finger and turn on Billie Holiday to wait for Saturday. By Saturday, I'm usually ok. There's stuff to do on Saturday. And Sunday is getting ready for Monday.

I pour another round and wait for Saturday. It's probably too much but I'll sleep tonight.

On Saturday mornings, we would go down the hill to the bakery for coffee and muffins. They had good blueberry muffins. We would talk. I guess I talked. She never talked much. Maybe that was the thing.

I found out from one of her friends that the bastard in my shoes wasn't anybody special. At first, I thought he might be a manager at a studio or an executive. Turned out he worked at our grocery store.

They said he was a produce manager. Figure that one. I gave her three months of that before she moved on. She lived larger than he would ever be.

When she moved over to Burbank, I tried to find her but it felt creepy, slipping through parking lots like a stalker. After January, I decided it was time to move on so I stopped going over there. I don't know where she is anymore.

I check the faces in the store but I haven't seen her yet. After she ditched him, she probably moved somewhere else. Santa Monica is more her speed. When I'm driving around Burbank I wonder what I would do if I ever found her.

Probably nothing, I'm doing ok now. I'm saving my money for a trip to Europe, maybe even Russia. Last night I got this email from a person named Margo. From the way she writes, I think she might be Russian.

Hi my Dear Stranger!

I'm very young and energetic lady! I have very positive attitude to life and people. I do enjoy new experience life can offer me: to see new interesting places, to meet new people.

I do try to enjoy every moment of life and accept everything way it comes without complaining.

Though my life seems to be quite enjoyable there's one important missing thing. It's LOVE!

Without my beloved one, my soul mate, my King my life is not completed. I wish could find him very soon so that we share together some moment of the lifetime romance!

What about you? Could be my King? If answer yes - you find more about me at http://my.soulmate.com

au revoir,

Margo

It's probably fake, but you never know. I printed it out before I deleted it, just in case. Margo is a good name. Margo makes me think of *The Shadow*.

I wonder if love is a different dimension, a super string like gravity that vibrates at a different rate from the rest of life.

- Cocobolo -

Sex Life of Ghosts

I

My great-great-grandmother was Cherokee. After I moved to Los Gatos, I dreamed about her. In my dreaming, my great-great-grandmother would turn on my TV and watch soap operas.

At the time, I did not know who she was.

She was an old woman, kept her hair coiled in silver plaits around her head. Sometimes she wore her plaits like twin snakes running down her back. She always wore a long sleeved brown dress with a lace-trimmed collar, buttoned up to her throat. A dress, long and covering her ankles. Sometimes she wrapped herself in an old quilt. February night was cold and I had no heater in the room.

The first time I saw her sitting in my chair I asked, "Who are you?"

I was dreaming and did not know her then.

She laughed and said, "Osiyo, Edward. Tohitsu?"

It was only a dream so I was not afraid. In the dream, I just stayed in bed and looked at her. It was strange, the way that dreams are.

I said, "I don't understand."

She watched me with black eyes. "You know little." And the dream ended.

One night she sat in my chair and sang songs to me. Her voice was soft and came from deep in her throat. She would sit in my chair, smoke cigarettes, and tell me stories. I could not understand what she was saying.

When I asked, "Who are you?" she said, "Nasgi utsi ulisi."

In my dreams, I thought she meant fairy godmother, which was strange because she did not have wings. But, dreams are always strange so I accepted it for what it was.

I told her, "I don't understand."

She watched me with black eyes. "You know little," she said and the dream ended.

My dreams about the old woman were like that. She would sit in my chair and say things or sing small songs I did not understand. She watched reruns on my TV and smoked cigarettes. In my dream, she would turn the air blue with smoke and the smell of tobacco would linger in my nose for days.

The next day I would wake up and try to figure out what the dream songs meant while I drank my first coffee and watched the news. Dreams are like that. Sometimes they hang around with you all day while you puzzle over bits of them. That is how life is.

In the mornings, I would pour a cup of coffee and sit on the upstairs porch outside my room. Spring weather in Los Gatos was mild. Usually it was a nice day, blue sky, a bit of breeze. Morning in spring was almost too cool. Morning coffee was good in spring and fall.

Spring was as fall. Winter was too short to be a season. Summer was the only other season.

In the foothills, where I lived it was stifling hot in the summer. On late summer mornings while the air was still cool, my landlady swept fallen olive leaves from the driveway. I sat in shade behind the trellis on the upstairs porch and watched her sweep. With every breeze, they dropped from the tree's canopy and littered the concrete. She worked the broom from side to side, head down and focused on the dead knife blade leaves. Her curly gray hair, bunched up on her head in a puff by a soiled tennis visor. Garden gloves covered her hands.

She did not see me.

Her name was Alice Watson. She lived alone. Her husband died in a war. I never asked which one. When I first met her she just said, "The war." After that, I never talked to her except to say hello and hand her the rent. She would work in the yard until lunch and then disappear inside her house.

That was the only time I saw her during the day.

Sometimes at night, I would hear her TV when I got home from work. I could hear it from outside her window. She watched a Catholic channel on cable. I could hear them saying, "Hail Mary, full of grace. The Lord is with thee." That was all I knew about her.

I rented a room behind Alice Watson's old house on Bachman Avenue. It was upstairs over the garage with a small kitchen counter and space for a bed, a chair, and my writing desk. I bought a TV at a garage sale down the street and put it on my desk. It was one of those little TVs people used to take with them on trips in their cars. Now everybody has DVD players.

Los Gatos was an hour south of San Francisco but it reminded me of the town where I grew up only nicer. I liked Los Gatos. Except, in Los Gatos houses cost about twelve times what my dad's did. I think real estate developers invented California. Only rich bastards could afford to buy a good house. Everybody else just rented. They believed they would buy a house someday and get rich too. I didn't understand their thinking. They would never be rich. They were going nowhere like me. The bank would always own their house.

I had a job at Daryl D's. Daryl D's was a sports bar and grill on Santa Cruz Avenue. Every day except Thursday, I mixed drinks and poured beers. Every afternoon at three, I left my apartment. I walked down the street to the bar. Inside Daryl D's, I stepped behind the bar and put on the apron. I split the bar with Bobby. He was the other bartender. He had the end of the bar by the door. I had the end by the restaurant.

Sometimes down at my end a customer wanted to sit and have a meal with their drink. I had to take their food order and serve dinner like I was a waiter. I hated that. Bar tips were mine and I did not split them. On food orders, I had to split tips on meals with the kitchen crew.

First thing I did every day was wipe down the bar. I wiped the bar until it looked like glass. I never wiped Bobby's half though. He did not care. He said nobody could tell in the dark. Some people are like that.

At night, I poured drinks. I poured tequila shooters for programmers, wine for middle-aged women wearing jewelry, makeup, and perfume. I poured JD and coke for old guys. They hit on every woman in the place. I mixed daiquiris for blue-jeaned girls. I watched for the daiquiris and tequila shooters. Tips made my rent. They tipped the best.

Daryl D's closed at midnight. After cleanup, I walked back to my apartment. It was usually 2AM. The streets were dead at 2AM. Only streetlights and traffic lights worked that late. Streetlights made black shadows on the sidewalks. I enjoyed walking through them. In yards where tree leaf canopies stretched, you could not see your hand in front of your face.

At night when I walked home, I wondered if the old woman would visit. When I walked, I whispered Yes, No, Yes, No. I did that like when I was a kid and we pulled petals off flowers to read the future. Sometimes she did. Sometimes she did not. She had no pattern. Divining her arrival never worked. Some nights I was tired of her TV shows and singing and story telling. Those nights I slept with the covers pulled over my head and ignored my dreaming her.

And so it went through the summer.

In September, on the ninth, I called my grandmother to wish her happy birthday. She was over 100 but did not want to be reminded of her age. She did not want to die. If I did not call, though, she would feel hurt. All morning I sat in my room thinking about what I would say to her. My gut turned into a knot. When I called her, I said hello and asked how she was feeling.

That worked. We talked about arthritis and glaucoma for an hour. When she said arthritis did not let her sleep at night, I told her about a medicine I saw on a news report. She told me that Old Forrester was her medicine. Then I told her about the old woman who was in my dreaming.

My grandmother said, "That must be Grandma Going. She's talking to you in Cherokee."

I did not know Cherokee. I asked her, "Are we Indian?"

She laughed. Her laugh was like short breath. She sounded like the old woman in my dreaming.

"No. That was too long ago." She said, "Look in the mirror. There's no Cherokee left in you."

She was right. I was English pasty white. I burned in the sun and never tanned. Blond hair and blue eyes, any Cherokee had washed out of me.

"What does she want, Mammaw?"

"You have to ask her."

"She won't speak English."

"Then learn Cherokee," my grandmother breathed softly. I heard her through the telephone.

The next day, I went to the library. The library in Los Gatos is not very big. They ordered a Cherokee vocabulary book for me and I tried to learn. Nothing stuck. The words and sounds slipped in and out of my head like sand. I covered my ears when I spoke. I tried to hold the sounds inside but they disappeared as I said them.

In those weeks, my great-great-grandmother did not visit so I could not practice what I tried to learn. It was crazy anyway. She was a dream, a Blue Agave invocation.

Days later, one night in my dreaming, I smelled her cigarettes. She smoked strong tobacco, perique. It was a dark smell, sweet and bitter at once, stinging deep in my sinuses. I opened one eye to see if it was her. She laughed and blew a smoke cloud at me.

I sat up and asked her, "Why are you here?"

"Osiyo, Edward. Tohitsu?"

She looked at me, her eyes were black marbles sunk into cupped sockets and wrinkled hickory nut leather. The glitter reflection of the TV screen gave them surface.

"Osiyo, Grandmother." I had remembered how to say hello. "I'm doing fine. Tohitsu?"

"I am well." She smiled without showing her teeth. That would be impolite. I learned that from a book at the library. "You know more," she said.

"Mammaw said I should learn to speak Cherokee."

She sat in my chair and blew smoke clouds into the air. "You have a small room."

"I don't make much money. I'm just a bartender. It costs a lot to live here."

"Why?"

"It's California."

She stared at me.

"Silicon Valley," I said. "Many people want to live here. The weather is good. There are many jobs."

She stared at me without speaking. She was not interested in California. She waved her hand through the air and pointed at the TV. "This is disgraceful." She was watching All My Children again. She always watched that soap. I never understood why.

I told her, "You should watch another station."

"No. This is interesting." She blew a cloud of blue at my TV. "These people are fools," and she laughed softly.

I did not say anything else while she smoked and watched the soap opera. And the dream ended.

One night while she was watching All My Children I asked her, "What clan are we?" I had been going to the library reading about the Cherokee.

She said, "I am Anitsisqua." She smoked her cigarette before she said, "The bird clan. You are of no clan. There are no clans in the People today."

In my dream, anguish overwhelmed me. It clamped my throat closed and locked my chest. My eyes filled with tears. Emotions in dreams are deep. I could not speak.

And the dream ended.

I woke up. I had cried in my sleep. Emotions in dreams are deeper than in real life.

I drank my coffee on the upstairs porch and thought about the feeling of the dream. That feeling stayed with me through afternoon and into the evening.

One night in October, my great-great-grandmother told me a story. It was about the Sun and the Moon. She said when they were young, Moon noticed Sun with her warmth and beauty. Not knowing Sun was his sister in the Universal Circle, Moon sat near her each day to seek her favor. When evening came, Moon hurried away. One day Sun said to Moon, "I want to touch your face." Moon refused and moved away from Sun. Before Moon could leave, Sun threw ashes on his face. When Moon was bright in the evening sky, Sun saw the ashes on his face. Knowing that Moon was her brother in the Universal Circle, Sun never came close to him again. Today, Mother Earth sits between Sun and Moon.

She smoked her tobacco. I did not know what else to say after her story. I didn't understand what it meant. I was embarrassed to ask. The silence was uncomfortable.

"Where is your wife," she asked.

I said. "Los Angeles. She went back to her family."

"Why are you still here?" she asked.

I could not speak. My throat clamped shut until it hurt. And the dream ended.

I opened my eyes. It was morning. I fixed coffee and sat on the porch outside my room. Downstairs, my landlady swept fallen olives from her driveway. They had shriveled black.

When I lived in Los Angeles, I had an olive tree at my house. One year I cured olives and gave them as Christmas presents to Salley's parents. Her parents smiled and thanked me. Salley's mother held the jars from her when taking them into her kitchen. In spite of her smile, she did not want them. The olives did not come from a deli.

L.A. was a forgotten life.

I finished my coffee.

After we moved to San Jose, Salley went back to L.A. She could not live away from her family.

I took my empty cup inside my apartment and called my grandmother. In our conversation, I told her about the dreams and stories. I asked why Grandma Going was in Louisiana and not Oklahoma with other Cherokee.

Mammaw said, "They slipped away before the soldiers came." Mammaw said, "They never talked about being Cherokee.

They never spoke Cherokee. They wanted to disappear. They wanted to be left alone."

   "Oh," was all I said. I was hollow to hear they had disappeared. After that, we talked about arthritis until I had to leave for work. I promised I would call back another day and tell more about my dreaming.

II

One night, when it was Fall, a blond headed woman came into Daryl D's. She was wearing a cream-colored pants suit, gold rings, bracelets, and necklace. I smiled friendly at her and she sat at my end of the bar. She looked like she had money. Bobby never acted friendly. He had a girlfriend and didn't worry about rent. I needed the tip. Rent was in a week. I wiped my hands on my apron. "What can I get for you?" I smiled and leaned in to hear her. It was Sunday night and loud. The 49ers were playing.

"Glass of white wine." Flash of smile before her eyes moved away. The skin across her face was drum tight. Plastic surgery.

"House?" I pulled out a wine glass.

"That's fine." She moved her hand in air, "I'm just killing time until some friends get here." She turned toward a crowd at the door. "We're going to have dinner in the restaurant. Could you put this on my tab?" She held out her credit card. She had old hands. Women in Daryl D's were like that. Younger looked older. Older looked younger. I could not tell how old they were. Except for their hands.

She squirmed on the barstool. She was looking everywhere at once. I watched her swing one-way then the other. I make up stories about people at the bar. Divorced, first time out. I ran her card. It had a picture of a Siamese cat on it. One of those new cards that let you do that. If I had a card, it would have a horse on it, a thoroughbred like Secretariat. Or a bear.

I filled a glass and she reached to pick it up. "Thanks." She crossed her legs and sipped the wine. "Can you put the TV on the soccer game? The Quakes are playing tonight."

I looked at the bar TV. It was on bull riding. A cowboy was getting his face stepped on by a bull while it dragged him in the dirt. Professional bull riding, no one was watching. The Quakes were on a different satellite.

"I'll get the manager to change it. Be right back."

I cursed on the walk to the office. Sometimes I say stuff too fast. I never leave the bar cause Bobby gets my action. I wondered how much it was going to cost me. Rent was next week.

I told Terrell a lady wanted to watch the Quakes. He said, "Damn it, Edward." But he went to the satellite box anyway. It was a customer request. Back at the bar, three daiquiris were standing at my end. I might have missed more but I could not tell.

I told the woman, "Terrell's changing it for you."

"Thank you. I hate to be a bother but I just can't stand to watch that bull riding. Or football."

"It's no bother."

"My daughter used to play professional soccer." She leaned back and stretched with arched back and breasts round like honeydew melon. I looked at a dull spot on the bar and polished it. I did not need her distraction chasing inside my brain. There was no salvation from Daryl D's. There was no celestial benevolence. No easy out.

Recomposed, I glanced up. Unexpected lust was an illusion. A dream like great-great-grandmother's soaps, a sex life for ghosts. "Does she still play?"

The woman's eyes looked past me into the bar mirror. "No," Her tone turned condescending. "The league went under a couple of years ago. She had to get a real job."

"That's a shame. What's she doing now?" But she was done with me. The air was cold.

The woman waved to a couple at the door. She shouted their names.

Two people waved at her, squeezed their way to the bar.

The woman directed them to a bar table. She told them, "I'm going to watch the end of the Quakes game."

They smiled. "Of course."

She ordered two glasses of house white for them.

I opened a Chablis and poured the wine. She chattered to them the same story she told me, "My daughter used to play professional soccer."

While I watched, I arranged glasses behind the bar. They worked with the woman, small office. Gold jewelry. Expensive clothes. They sold real estate in the valley. They drove BMWs. It was her business. They let her boss them around. She was their boss. Their story wasn't interesting and I left it unfinished.

Three guys wanted refills, whistled, and raised their glasses. I left to pour shooters and JD. When I returned, she was talking with an old guy, fifties or sixties. I didn't recognize him. He wasn't a regular.

He had his chest out saying his sons played football like him. Quarterbacks like him. Slick, wearing a Burberry shirt and pleated khaki slacks. He had precision cut hair; dyed jet black next to tanned skin: A tech company exec, a startup stock millionaire, or venture capitalist. He was a VC king. People in the valley treated them like gods. Before the bust, they believed they were gods.

I cleaned cocktail glasses and stacked them behind the bar. Half of bartending is washing away the remains of customers' drinks.

The real-estate woman told him real football was soccer.

The old guy backed off. He restarted his pitch telling her that his sons were into AYSO soccer when they were growing up. They would have stayed with it if there had been a soccer league.

She told him that her daughter had played professional soccer.

He came back with the World Cup was the only soccer league that mattered. He told her everything he thought he knew about the World Cup. He didn't know crap.

He was just making it up. She didn't know any better. Only thing she knew about soccer was her daughter played pro one time.

I wiped the bar down. In my brain, I told them about the Bundesliga. I pulled for Bayern München. The words stayed in my head. I was invisible to them. If I said words, they wouldn't hear me. My words would pass through them without stopping. I was the bartender. I picked up used glasses off the bar and cashed in tabs.

I tossed my bar rag into the bin and pulled out a clean one.

The Quakes lost. In that moment, the real-estate woman with her drones moved to the restaurant. They left the VC king in mid-sentence. He stood holding a scotch in his hand with a foot propped on the rung of the barstool. It happened fast. He looked like Washington crossing the Delaware. I laughed. I hoped he felt stupid.

Before he could feel alone, the VC king spotted another woman and moved on.

I wiped the bar and cleaned their glasses. That was the highlight of my night. Her tip was ok but not great. The rest of the evening was routine. I was glad when

Terrell said I could take off. That was about 10. Sunday slows down fast after the game ends.

The outside air was wet coming in over the mountains from Santa Cruz. It hung in space, a cloud not yet fog. Daryl D's door shut the noise inside the bar. Los Gatos was quiet and covered me, drew the bar noise out of my head. The streets slick black from wet. Drips of water fell off the roof edge. I hunched the jacket collar up on my neck and crossed Santa Cruz.

I saw the VC king walking with the real-estate woman. They were across the street with her trying to get to her car. Her friends were gone already. It was just her. He was rambling to her about his kids playing soccer. The man kept a death grip on the only line he had. She was pushing buttons on her key fob until the lights on a silver Mercedes winked and the car chirped.

He was not giving up, leaning on a wall to stand while he talked World Cup.

I thought I never looked like that, even on my dark days. Mostly, I kept to my room. I did not bother people if I could help it. That is how I was raised. Each day I came down the stairs and did my job. On weekends, I went to the store and bought food. Early mornings I sometimes walked through town and looked in store windows at displays. That was just killing time. I never wanted what they sold. And after each time out, I went back home and up the stairs. Thursday nights I might go to the bar up the street and drink. The Scot Tartan was a dark place. That was it. I don't recall using a wall to hold me up when I walked out.

"Is that drunk bothering you, ma'm?" I shouted.

She glanced from me to the VC king. "No. I guess not."

She wouldn't pull the plug on her own kind. I should have left when she said that. I was the wine dispenser. I was a daiquiri maker and JD blender. I could have, should have, left her with the drunk. But I wasn't raised that way. I stepped quick and fast across the street to grip the old man's arm. Under the cloth, it was shriveled muscle on bone. I felt the chord of it running elbow to shoulder.

The VC king was surprised and stumbled.

I told him, "I can call a cab for you, bud."

He shouted, "Go to hell," and staggered back against the wall.

I laughed at him.

The real-estate woman slipped away. I heard tires chirp and she was gone. I said he was a drunk bastard. I watched his face twist up. We had a barn cat did that when the dog came around. Hissing and spitting till the dog left it.

I started walking down Santa Cruz to my room. Laughing. He could get his own ride home. I was *me* again for a minute. It was good to be back in my skin after so long on the skids. I took two steps toward Bachman Avenue. Laughing at the old guy was probably a mistake. Walking away from him was another mistake; that, and calling him a drunk. I never heard him behind me. All I remember was seeing yellow sparkles and feeling sidewalk with my face, thinking on my way down that I was stupid and careless.

III

I smelled Grandma Going's cigarettes and opened my eyes. She was sitting on a bench at the bus stop. She laughed loud and said, "Osiyo. Tohitsu?"

"Osiyo, Grandmother." I sat up. I put my hand on the back of my head where the bastard hit me. "My head hurts tonight." I had a lump growing that was the size of a golf ball. "What are you doing out here?"

"Waiting for you. You should climb out of that gutter. It's embarrassing." She looked away from me so that I would not be ashamed and smoked her cigarette until I managed to stand. "You should know better than turn your back on a drunk man. They are like wild dogs."

My head was killing me. She walked with me toward the apartment, smoking her cigarettes, talking about drunken men and wild dogs.

I listened and said, "Yes, ma'm" when she finished each lesson.

We crossed the street at the corner of Bachman and Santa Cruz. She said, "I would like to tell you a story about little wren."

"Yes, grandmother." I pressed on the lump at the back of my skull. "I enjoy your stories."

She said, "Little wren is the messenger of the birds. She pries into everything. She gets up early in the morning and goes to every house in the village to gather news for the bird council. When a new baby is born, she finds out if it is a boy or girl and reports to the council. If it is a boy, the council sings a mournful chorus. Alas! The sound of the arrow! You see, the birds know that when the boy is older he will hunt them and kill them and roast them on a stick. If the baby is a girl, they are glad and sing. Thanks! The sound of the pestle! The birds know at her home they can gather stray grain where she grinds corn into meal."

She loved to tell me stories like that. I asked, "What does it mean, Grandmother?"

She dropped the end of her cigarette and crushed it with the toe of her shoe. "It is a story about the wren."

I did not say anything else. My head was killing me. A blood pulse pounded in my skull. It was going to explode. My stomach shrunk into my liver. I needed to vomit.

She said, "That man is weak. He ran away after he hit you."

I shrugged. "He was just a drunk from the bar. I didn't know him."

She held onto my arm as we walked.

"That woman was not for you," she said. "You needed someone in the heart."

"I don't want anyone anymore, Grandmother." I said, "I think I'm better off by myself."

She whispered, "Every day you know more. But it causes you trouble."

She walked with me down Bachman Avenue to the house and up the steps to my room. The first thing she did when we got inside was turn on my TV and watch All My Children. I kicked off my shoes and sprawled across the bed. She rolled another cigarette and lit it. I watched the room turn blue.

"Grandmother, why do you always watch this show?"

She did not say anything at first. I thought she was ignoring me, closed my eyes, and pulled a pillow over my head.

In a moment she said, "It shows something that only happens for the living. People wanting each other."

Outside my window, there was laughing in the parking lot next door. The Irish pub was closing. High-pitched girl shrieks and boy shouts, car doors slammed, and tires squealed across asphalt.

She said, "I like to see people want each other. "

I asked, "Even if it's disgraceful?" I tried to tease her.

She said, "Even if it is only in this pretend world. It reminds me of life and desire. That is all we have. That is all that's real."

I opened my eyes. She was gone and the sun was up. It was almost noon but the TV was still on, The Young and the Restless this time. Somebody named Victor was upset that a woman named Abby was moving in with a guy named Brad.

I turned the set off, slipped on my sandals, and staggered into the bathroom to take a handful of supersized Tylenol. My head was still killing me. I felt the lump on the back of my skull. It was bigger.

"Bastid," popped out of my mouth. I recalled, out of nowhere, a kid in St. Helena called us bastids when we picked on him.

I remembered. His name was Finnegan.

His family moved to St. Helena from New York.

We made fun of him.

His mother was Italian and his dad was Irish.

He had black curly hair and dark skin.

He didn't look like a Finnegan.

We picked on him all of the time.

He didn't belong in St. Helena.

His sister was beautiful.

I used to punch him until he cried.

His sister cried for him.

His sister was beautiful.

Anguish overwhelmed me. I rubbed my eyes dry. Washed my face and hands. Can't wash away sins. I tried to not remember them but time caught me out. Memory is what ghosts are. Pain, love, desire.

I fixed a cup of espresso and sat outside on the stairs to my room.

It was a nice fall day, blue sky, a bit of breeze.

In St. Helena where I was born, fall was a cool relief. The air turned from sweltering summer to dry cool. The light changed from glare to bright and charged the air with expectation of joy. Winter would be a wet cold, soaking into your bones. And spring was its warm respite. Living here so long in this place, I had forgotten why rain and summer heat were good.

Downstairs, my landlady swept the fallen olives from her driveway, working the broom from side to side, head down and focused on the little green and black mottled bodies.

I watched Alice Watson sweep fallen olives. She did not see me sitting upstairs.

I called down, "Nice day, isn't it."

Alice Watson looked up and shielded her eyes from the sky.

- Cocobolo -

Hydroformed

Shouting in the room next door snapped him out of the dream. It had been a good one too. He was on a motorcycle. A new Harley, a VROD, 20 grand, 115 fuel-injected horses, liquid cooled, hydroformed frame, and slash tipped pipes. The motorcycle was a part of him. And he was riding fast flowing like mercury around corners and over hills. Getting the light feeling in his gut and chest when he topped a hill and dropped over the other side, with the pipes stretched out behind him channeling high-speed thunder across the world that he passed through, like a god of war, he flowed effortless down the PCH. But it wasn't like any part of the PCH he'd ridden. There was no Pacific coast, no ocean, and the highway was a two-lane country road; nothing like cutting through Malibu or Santa Monica. And then the road ended. Stopped dead at a barricade of posts and steel railing. He stopped the motorcycle at the barrier and there were eucalyptus trees growing in a thick line behind the posts with bark shredded and hanging from smooth brown bones. Behind the row of trees might have been a green field and farther back maybe some hills. But the important part was the motorcycle was heavy as a dead body he heaved and struggled to turn inside the little space of the two-lane road. And he wanted that freedom back, fast gliding over the road, that flowing high-speed rush, he wanted it. Which is about the time that the shouting next door woke him. And then the thumpthumpthump on the wall and the woman's voice going ohbabyohbaby too long for him to get back to the ride down PCH somewhere back in California. And then silence.

Goddamn sumbitches.

He wanted to put his fuckin' fists through the wall and choke the living shit out of them. He was staring at the ceiling. The streetlight outside lit up his room in blue mercury. He reached over for his cell phone.

2:31 AM in LCD black.

He picked the crushed pack of Picayunes from the table by the bed and went out the front door. It was a warm night for December. That was New Orleans, one night 75 and then a cold front the next day could drop it to 27. But the cold never lasted. And its rain was always warm to him. In a smooth motion, he shook out a cigarette and pulled it from the pack with the corner of his mouth. A habit he picked up from Papa Goings. He was the one that stuck Jimmyboy on him for a name until his friends cut it down to JB. The old man told him, "Anybody actually worked for a living wouldn't go putting their fingers on a cigarette butt they were going to put in their mouth."

JB looked down in the motel parking lot where his bike was leaking oil. A 79 Shovelhead, straight pipes and heavy miles on the frame, nothing like his dream. It was a piece of junk, but it was his piece of junk.

He pulled the old Zippo lighter out of the pocket of his jeans and flipped it open. Couldn't do that with those plastic Bics. Snapped the cover closed after he got the first drag. It was heavy. Globe and anchor, the old man packed that thing all over Korea during the war. The chrome worn off at the edges with the brass underneath polished smooth, he slipped it back in his pocket.

One more day of this joint. He turned and checked the room next door. The light was on. By the start of the second Picayune, the girl stepped out, still working her way back into her tight black leather skirt.

Hey hon, she saw him standing by the railing. You lookin' lonely tonight.

I'm cool.

She stopped in mid-stride, cocked one hip higher than the other, knee pointing out toward the parking lot, skinny body balanced on platform shoes. Wanta go on a date?

JB waved her off. Not this trip.

Comon hon. Just a little date. She slowly fanned the dark morning with her leg, twisting it on the pivot of her heel. What do you say? Something to help you relaaax. She drew the a's out like a cat using all the breath in her lungs.

JB turned his back and waved her off again. Two things about whores learned early on was don't waste time arguing with them and don't believe that oh-baby-oh-baby shit.

After a minute of wheedling, she snorted, called him a bastid, and clopped down the narrow balcony to the stairs.

He watched her walk on the platforms and wondered how she kept from falling. She made the corner at the stairwell and was gone. He was wide-awake now. Maybe he should have said, sure babe, but he couldn't risk getting busted right now. He stretched, reached an arm out, and flexed the muscles in his forearm. He liked to do that. It made the tattooed snakes on his arms come alive. Cheap thrill. The muscles in his forearms moved like a rat bulge going up the snake's gut. They were good tats. Got 'em done at a parlor in Monterey when he was up there once running some shit for a buddy in L.A., Alexy Kuznetkof. Alex got himself whacked last week.

JB spat off the balcony.

Alex kept him out of trouble. Alex deserved better. He was a good man.

JB exhaled a smoke line and rubbed his eyes with the balls of his thumbs. He liked Monterey. Eating in places on the bay. Had a few drinks and lunch at the same place where Eastwood ate lunch with that woman in the Play Misty movie. And tattoo places, it used to be a sailors town. It had to have tattoo places.

The guy that did the snakes knew his stuff. Did them so their tails wrapped around his neck and coiled down both of his arms, copperheads twisting like the real thing with the heads tattooed on his fists. When he clinched 'em, that's all anybody saw, copperheads. Right after he got the snakes done, he was over in Fresno and got into it with this guy in one of those California redneck joints. That was the first time he'd really seen what they looked like. His fists were giant fuckin copperheads. Sick.

He smoked out his cigarette and flipped the butt over the rail. A couple of cops flew down the side street, blue and white cars in New Orleans, baby blue, light bars flashing. He watched them for a second but they were headed somewhere else.

He could smell the swamp rot in the air. Tourists didn't know what it was, didn't like it. It smelled like mold and fungus. One time he heard a woman at the airport say that when she was coming off a jet from Phoenix. In Arizona, there was nothing to smell. In New York, all he smelled was city funk. Maybe the air was the best part of New Orleans. Every odor in the world swirled in that soup.

He went back into the room and poured two fingers of Glenlivet, switched on the TV and sat on the bed. He checked his cell phone, 3:10AM. Waiting for dawn.

He checked the channel guide: Paid Programming; Meet the Press; Shepherd's Chapel; and Globe Trekker. Globe Trekker looked ok. On the remote, he pushed Info. Cuba and Haiti. Forget that shit. CSPAN2, Book TV, Book Events. That ought to put him to sleep. He pushed 2 3. Some woman was doing an interview with a prick about Eudora Welty. Blah blah blah.

One finger of 'livet gone. Tomorrow night he'd be back on the road, Pensacola. All he needed was Paulo's bag.

One time when he was a kid, Dad took them down past Pensacola on a vacation. First time he'd ever seen turquoise water. It looked fake. The old man said it was real. Said it was like that all the way down to the Keys. The old man was an asshole so he didn't believe him. Later when he was seventeen he ditched school, St. Helena, that little crap town he grew up in, and headed for the Keys. Asshole was right about that water.

3:30 AM. Second finger of 'livet gone.

JB reached his arm out and set his glass on the table by the bottle. He hadn't been back to St. Helena since. Even though he was sitting here an hour away, he wouldn't go up that road. He was lucky to get out of there when he did.

He lit another cigarette. Opened and closed the lighter, he felt the snap of the heavy metal cover jolt into his finger bones.

Twelve years on the road running shit for guys and still breathing. Couldn't ask for more than that.

By sunup he was asleep.

He turned the key and thumbed the starter switch. The two-cylinder thump rumbled windows in the cheap rooms. In the next movement, he was rolling out of the parking lot into night traffic. He had the bag draped across the rear fender. He didn't know what was in it. He didn't care. Another run was all it was. The only thing that really mattered was getting it to Pensacola and getting his money.

All afternoon he'd been waiting for the drop. Sitting on his ass going nowhere gave him the jumps. When the car arrived, he was ready and stepped across the parking lot, but careful not to look too hurried, nothing unusual, just a guy walking past a car. Paulo passed the package through the window and everybody split. No burning rubber or wild assed driving, just a smooth handoff and no talking, no waiting around, Paulo ran a smooth crew.

JB left New Orleans. Two and a half hours straight to Mobile, then down through the tunnel under the river, the sound of his pipes ripping off the ceramic tile tunnel walls, and up across the top of the bay. Another hour to Pensacola, keeping it down to 65, no cutting loose, no crazy shit until he got the bags delivered. He was a pro, he always delivered, and he kept his mouth shut. Not like the new boys some of the guys were using. Punks and Ninja bikes, a couple of Cuervos and they were shooting their mouths off about running this or that, leaving cops stupid on side streets. They wouldn't last long. They had no code.

10 PM and south on 110 to Cervantes, he hooked a right on North E. Dead ahead was the Baptist Hospital. Nobody but Fat Jack would have thought about using a Baptist Hospital. He was a wicked humor. JB rode into the front parking lot looking for the fat man and spotted the Escalade. JB stopped his bike three rows back, picked up the saddlebag, and started walking for the Emergency Room watching the Escalade from the corners of his eyes. Eddy Grigo stepped down from Fat Jack's Escalade and crossed over to walk with him. Eddy was Fat Jack's legs and would do the transfer away from him, in case

something went wrong. If shit happened, Fat Jack would ease out of the parking lot as if he didn't know either of them. That was the way.

"Jimmyboy," Eddy smiled wide, big teeth, dark face, "got a present for you," and passed an envelope as they walked. Eddy called him Jimmyboy to piss him off.

Slick Eddy dressed in Tommy Bahama silk shirts and pants. The New Yorker in Florida look, JB knew Eddy carried a stiletto in his baggy pants pocket, ready to whip it on him in a heartbeat. Eddy was a freak. Last month Eddy tried to stick him on a delivery, thought he could lift his fee. Legs tried to do that sometimes. Thought nobody would care if a runner dropped off the list. Eddy claimed he was just playing him. JB knew it was a lie. Eddy was still itching to stick him. JB saw it in the way Eddy rolled his thumb across the inside pads of his fingers and grinned. Doing the drop without getting buried was the tricky bit.

As they walked up to the hospital, JB opened the envelope, took out the plastic card and the slip with the PIN. While Eddy bought a candy bar from a vending machine, JB ran the card through the bank machine, saw the money was there, pulled out the max allowed and stuffed the envelope in his hip pocket. They stepped out and on the sidewalk shielded from security cameras, JB set the saddlebag on the concrete, and lit up a Picayune, never taking his eye from Eddy.

"You don't like me, Jimmyboy?" Eddy grinned like a prick.

"I don't care one way or the other about you, Tommy Bahama." JB watched the eyes, waited on the twitch at the corners that came before the knife leaped into the open. "I don't give a shit about you."

"Watch your step, JB." Eddy stared at him. "You're too old for this line of work." He took the package out of the saddlebag. "You should quit. Go back to California and your Russians. Let the little boys do this shit." Eddy walked with an easy pace back to the Escalade, not fast, not slow, nothing to look any different from anyone else leaving the hospital.

JB watched the fat arm take the package and candy bar from Eddy who slipped into the front seat and closed the door. The Escalade pulled away and JB leaned into the hospital wall, still alive, still free. He watched ambulances arrive and leave while he finished the Picayune, before he returned to the bike where he sat and held his money, felt the hard edges of the new bills, and the quarter inch stack before he transferred them to his wallet. He fired up the bike and let it thump against the air.

He wasn't that old.

He could still do the long rides as good as anybody.

Forty minutes out of Pensacola, he felt the snap, the engine rev, and the bike slow. The drive belt was gone, rattling on the belt guard. He rolled off the highway and onto the grass.

Coming out of the hospital parking lot, he'd screwed up, made a right on Cervantes instead of a left, and then decided it was good to ride back along the coast. Just like that vacation when he was a kid. Sentimental crap always got him in trouble. He should have just taken the interstate back to New Orleans. Now he was stuck out on a country road halfway between Pensacola and Mobile, in the middle of nowhere. The crazy part about the entire mess was that he hadn't seen the beach since he left the outskirts of Pensacola. He should have figured the road would take the high ground.

He put the kickstand down and sat on the bike.

Midnight and no traffic, at least it wasn't cold.

He dug his cell phone out of his vest and called roadside service. It was a little hard to describe where he was but they passed him through to Mobile and a local who eventually figured out that he had just crossed the bridge over Fish River but not yet reached Highway 98.

"You're east of Point Clear."

"Great, how soon can you get here?"

"First thing in the morning. I got a low hauler in Fairhope I can get down that way."

"So how do I get to a hotel? You going to leave me out here on the road?"

"You got any friends you can call?"

"Not in fuckin Alabama."

The phone was silent. "Hey, you there? Or did I lose you." Coverage had been cutting in and out the whole time they had been talking.

"If you need help, I can get it for you. But cussing on the phone ain't going to do it."

JB dropped the phone from his ear and looked out across shadow shapes of naked pecan trees. Over on a hill about a half-mile away was a cluster of homes. Big silhouettes of two story things with horse fences around them, 10, maybe 20 acres for each place, no way was he going to get any help from those places. Not this time of night...probably not any time of day.

"Shit." He put the phone back to his ear. "Yeah. I need help."

"Ok. There's a shop in Fairhope just north of you. They specialize in bikes like yours. Retro Choppers. I'll give Barry a call. He'll get you hooked up."

"How long?"

"Somebody'll be down to get you in a few minutes. Sit tight." The connection dropped and the phone was dead.

JB stuffed the phone back in his vest, lit up a Picayune and sat in the dark on his bike waiting for a ride into town. "At least the mosquitoes aren't bad here. Nothing like Louisiana."

After unloading his bike at the shop, the tow truck driver, dropped JB at a hotel near the bay. In fact, sitting on the edge of the bed the next morning, JB could see the bay through his window. He moved to a chair and watched pelican squadrons wheel over the water and piers and trees and let the bay air coming from the open window cover him. It was humid cool air that smelled of fish and algae and brackish water.

The hotel was an old two-story wooden block of windows and doors with balconies running around it on all sides. From the look of the framing it was turn of the century. JB pulled on his leathers and stepped out on the balcony. The trees towered over the motel and shaded the ground right out to the edge of the water. Sailboats, little boats, lurched over the tops of the waves headed out from shore dodging in and out among themselves. He decided they must be racing. In the distance, he could see the shadow of Mobile. He didn't realize it was so far away or the bay so wide.

He lit up a Picayune and watched the boats duck and dodge.

He wondered if he could enjoy living in a place where people sailed little boats out into the bay and back just to see who could do it fastest.

But they weren't very fast. Hell, he could out run them on a bicycle. Wasn't anything like a speedboat, couldn't figure out where they got their thrill from in one of those bay boats.

He flipped the cigarette butt over the balcony. He was ready for breakfast, something heavy, eggs over easy, bacon, and biscuits. Grits, he was in Alabama, they had to fix some good grits here. Last night, the driver said there was a good little restaurant in town. The little town perched high on a bluff behind the motel and above the bay. It was a good morning for a walk, cool so far and not much humidity.

JB sat at the counter in Jay's and ordered biscuits, eggs, bacon, and a bowl of grits. Cup of black coffee. The waitress behind the counter set a thick white china cup down in front of him and poured a stream of coffee into the cup before she went back to the kitchen with his order. Around him, people talked about people in town, the news that never got in a paper. Sun flooded through the windows and across the floor. The girl at the cash register talked to people by their names. He drank the coffee and listened for each voice.

St. Helena might be like this but he did not remember. Other things were what he remembered about St. Helena.

Time moved slow for a change and he drank two cups of coffee before his order came steaming on a heavy oval white china platter. He cut up the eggs with his knife and fork making a chopped mess of dark yellow and white. Took the knife and sliced open the biscuits, steam rising from the fluffy white insides, stuffed them with butter.

His great grandmother made a different kind of biscuit, in a Dutch oven on the stovetop, they had a leathery skin and soft insides, a *dumpfbrot*. When he was little he didn't care for them so much, they weren't how biscuits looked on TV. Then he got older. He asked her how she made them and she said it wasn't anything special, just biscuits.

She was dead now and he never had biscuits like them since.

The woman that took his order stopped on a trip around the room and asked if he needed anything else. "No, ma'm," he said and she smiled as she placed his check on the counter. He smiled back and saw she had nice eyes, lines faint in their corners, she was pushing forty but not quite there. He said, "That was real good."

"Glad you liked it," she said over her shoulder as she moved to the other end of the counter to refill an old man's coffee cup. The old man could've passed for Papa

Goings if he was still alive. He had the creased face and big hands, working hands.

JB finished off the eggs and bacon, wiped down the plate with the biscuit, ate it, and emptied the coffee cup. He left a tip and paid his check. The girl at the cash register smiled and said, "Hope you have a good day today, sir."

He smiled back, "You too." He started toward the door and stopped, "My name's Jim. Nobody calls me sir. I'm not that old."

She grinned back and said, "Alright, Jim."

Jim Goings walked down the sidewalk, under the awnings and shade trees, past the old brick fronts of two story buildings, antique stores, and hardware stores. He had nowhere that he had to go and took his time. He had called Paulo last night after he got to the motel. The package had arrived, that was the only thing Paulo wanted to know.

He told Paulo about his bike breaking down and that was alright with him. There was nothing hot happening. No more obligations, yet.

Today, in the sun, he could go anywhere, do anything.

The sidewalk slanted down after a couple of blocks and the avenue narrowed into a street covered in shade from lines of arching oaks and the street curved back down to the bay. He was used to Louisiana towns that crept around water or perched in hollowed out sections of marsh grass, seldom more than a man's height above a flat Gulf.

He walked the street down the bluff to the town pier and stood out at its end looking across the bay to the distant shape of Mobile. He listened to the slap of waves on the pilings, the plunk of a fish snapping a bug off the water's mirror. He let time drain away.

The bay boat regatta fought its way back to shore and disappeared around a point. He figured they were headed into a marina somewhere up the shoreline and wondered who won.

Over the bay, to the distant north, white clouds collided and swirled inside each other, turning into columns of convoluted grey and purple, mesmerizing, they built themselves into bulbous black towers, streaming indigo rain from their bases as they passed over water onto land. Jagged lightening bolted from the clouds to the ground, gold yellow streaks of electric fire.

He stood on the pier and watched it all until the line of clouds lost their form and became haze.

Morning was gone and afternoon began. The sun baked him in the leathers and vest. The black boots steel toes held his feet to the ground and the walk back up the 60-foot bluff to town was longer than the walk down.

When he returned to the street of stores, the window in a little place called Surf City stopped him with a display of shirts, shorts, hats, and sandals. Similar to, but not quite, Eddy Grigo's wardrobe, not as flashy. The shirts were cotton not silk. The patterns were silhouettes in gouache not paintings in exotic colors. If he had to shed his leathers, that was more his style.

He turned a worn brass handle on the door beside the display window and stepped into the store. Naked brown wood floorboards flexed and creaked under his feet. It was a long narrow room in ancient brick with pattern stamped tin sheets covering its ceiling fifteen feet or more above his head, dark with lights hanging from the ends of electric cords dropped from junction boxes mounted in intervals on the tin sheet ceiling. He decided there must have been fans hanging from them in the old days before air conditioning. The hollowness of the open room sucked up sound and enforced quite for no reason other than its design.

The girl behind the counter looked up and asked if she could help him, was he looking for something in particular. She was a looker, black hair, ice blue eyes, wearing a skin tight Surf City t-shirt.

"Nothing particular. Something cool in this heat. And not flashy."

The girl looked him up and down. "Shirts or what."

"Everything: shirts, shorts, sandals. The whole shootin' match."

"Tommy Bahama's on that rack over there, Key West over there. Back in the corner are the Guayaberas."

"Thanks. I'll just look around for now. What're Guayaberas?"

"Cuban shirts. Let me know if I can help you."

JB picked some Key West shirts and shorts off the rack.

"Where can I try these on?"

The sales girl pointed in the back at a curtain stretched across the wall. "Oz."

"Oz?"

She grinned at him and then he got it. "Cute." He scowled. He didn't like looking foolish. And still she laughed. He decided she was a kid and ignored her.

JB changed into the new clothes and walked out carrying his leathers, vest, and boots. He could feel the cool air in the store move through the cloth and, looking at the snakes wrapped around his arms, he considered buying a long sleeved shirt but the air felt good on his arms.

"How do I look? Not too fancy?" He didn't want to look like Eddie Griego.

"Just right. Ready for the beach. You need some sandals now."

"What do you have?"

"All kinds but I think these Tevas suit you. You don't look like a beach clog guy. Not with all that mustache and sideburns. What size do you wear"? She walked around the counter and headed for a rack of shoes.

"11 or 12"

"Try these." She passed him a box. "And you need a hat. The sun will eat you up if you don't wear a hat." She handed him a Shady Brady that looked crushed and sweated in but flexed like skin.

JB slipped his feet into the sandals and wiggled his toes. It was strange, not wearing boots. He always wore boots. When he first started running he'd seen a runner wearing sneaks get his foot ripped off crashing out on a barricade. After that he always wore boots. Can't shift without feet. "Feels good."

"You didn't strike me as an accountant." She walked back to her counter. "They come in here sometimes, wearing full leathers and do-rags, but they're still accountants and lawyers. Just on vacation. I can spot 'em. They always walk like they have money, eat in restaurants, and tell people what to do."

"I don't?"

"No. You want that gear?"

"Sure. How much do I owe you."

"210.14 with tax."

JB handed her the bankcard and she ran it through the register. While he keyed in the PIN, he asked her what people in town did for fun at night. Where'd they go to have a good time.

She handed him his card. "There's an Irish pub a couple of blocks from here. It's called Blarney's. And a few doors down, there's The Joint. Looks like a place out of the French Quarter. Tourists go to The Pub."

"Where do you go."

"Blarney's." She looked him square in the face, "But you might be a bit old."

"I'm not that old yet. I just live hard. That's all."

"I see." She handed him a plastic bag. "You might want to put your things in here."

"Thanks." He rolled up his leathers and stuffed them in the bag. The girl handed him a second bag for his boots. "Guess I'll take these on back to the hotel."

"Where you staying?"

"A place called Bay Side."

"That's a nice place. How long?"

"A few days maybe. I don't know. My bike's in the shop."

"I see. It's a nice little town. Course if it gets too boring you can head into Mobile."

"Right now, quite is good." He slipped his sunglasses on and picked up his bags.

"Maybe I'll see you tonight at that Irish pub."

"Maybe."

"What's a good time to go over there?"

"5. After work."

"Sounds good. What's your name?"

"Susan."

"I'm Jim."

She watched him walk to the front door, snake tattooed arms carrying shopping bags. He heard her laugh again so without turning he lifted his right hand and gave her the finger before he opened the door and stepped onto the sidewalk. He heard her laugh harder and he grinned. She was tough.

Blarney's Irish Pub was a low roofed building on a backstreet of the village. It was set back from the street under the sweep of an oak tree's limbs and not easy to spot in the shadow. There was no blinking sign, no neon beer brand advertising in the windows. The only tipoff he had that it was the right place was a scattered cluster of empty bistro tables and Cinzano umbrellas on a patio with a modest Blarney's painted in green on an aqua wall. He walked up to the door, stepped into the air-conditioning, and waited for his eyes to adjust in the dim.

It was a small joint, 20 by 30 with a three sided bar in the middle of the space, leaving just enough room around the edge for bar tables and chairs. The stools around the bar were filled, the tables at the perimeter were empty.

JB sat at a table in the corner of the room and faced the bar.

"What can I get you?" The bartender had come around to the table and was standing there smiling like a lost friend.

"What'cha got?"

The bartender handed him a list of beers, no hard liquor, it was a pub not a bar, and JB told him "How about an Abita, the Turbo Dog. And some chips with salsa." He handed the beer list back and the guy was gone.

At the bar, two girls, he figured were bordering on 21, sat on the end huddled over a cell phone or something electronic. They were wearing fancy dresses and one of them had a tattoo sneaking out from under the back of her dress. He couldn't make out what it was, a chunk of ivy or a vine. Four guys were standing around the left end of the bar. One of them was wearing khaki shorts, white tee shirt and a canvas beach hat. The rest were decked out in jeans and polo shirts. They were all kids. JB took his hat off and put it on the table. The bartender showed up and put his beer bottle and a glass on the table.

"Chips and salsa will be out in a minute."

"Sounds good." JB poured his beer and let the foam build while he looked for the girl from the store. He spotted her sitting on the far side of the bar, talking to her friends, hand holding a glass, the other moving in the air, fingers poised in mid motion, flash of her teeth when she grinned. She was a wrinkle of light in the dark.

An old woman came out from a door in the back carrying a basket of chips and a bowl of red salsa. Her hair was died orange. He wondered why old people did that. He'd seen them in the stores, looking like clowns without costumes, though sometimes in costumes of violent colored pantsuits. The old woman would look better with white hair.

She set the basket and bowl on his table, "Here you go."

"Thank, you."

She went back through her door and he started in on the chips. They were organic whole grain chips and close to cardboard. The last thing he expected to get in an Alabama pub was baked multi-grain chips. It was like being in some sort of strange alternate universe. The salsa wasn't bad.

"I see you found the place," The girl had slipped away from her friends at the bar.

"Had a hell of a time. No neon lights or Jax Beer signs out front."

"Neighbors don't want that. It's just a little neighborhood place to go after work."

"I can see that."

"Folks here like things quiet. When they want loud they go over to the casinos in Mississippi." She took one of his chips and nibbled at an edge. "They have some good shows over there. You ever go?"

"No. I'm not a casino guy. Too easy to lose my ass in there."

"What about the shows. You go to those?"

"No. I'm a bit rough around the edges. I saw the billboards when I was coming across. Looks like its mostly old guys doing come backs."

"They're ok. I like to go. It's fun seeing them. Puts a face on the music I used to listen to. Doesn't cost much." She finished the chip and picked up another.

"Health food chips too. I wasn't expecting that."

"Low sodium and organic."

"Damn near thought I was in California for a minute. Got all dizzy."

"Too much sodium'll do that to you. That's why you should eat organic."

"Salsa is pretty good."

"Mrs. Kelley...."

"A good Irish name."

"She makes it herself."

"Was that her that brought it out?"

"Yeah. This is her place. She lived in Puerto Rico for a few years before she moved here. Makes a lot of Caribbean food. Sometimes she makes a black bean salsa that's got mango in it. I could just eat the salsa straight."

"Sounds good."

"What kind of bike do you have?"

"It's an old Harley."

"Figures. Matches you."

"I guess that was a complement."

"Sure. Where'd you get those tats. That's wild." She reached out and gripped his hand before he could move it back. That startled him.

"Monterey...out in California. That was a few years back."

She twisted it around so she could see the snakehead and then let it go. "You from California?"

"Louisiana. But I lived out there the last 10 years. LA mostly."

"What do you do?" She sipped her drink but studied him over the rim of her glass.

"Damn, girl." JB took a chip and dipped it into the salsa. He wanted time to think out what might be happening. He needed to slow down the questions. He didn't know this girl. Just met her in a clothing store. It wasn't smart to go talking about things to strangers. But she was a girl in the middle of nowhere Alabama. That couldn't hurt him. What could she say. Who could she tell if he slipped up.

He swallowed some beer and told her, "I deliver packages. Express stuff for some folks."

"I see." She ate another chip. "You on vacation?"

"For a few days. 'Kind of nice here. No big city noise. I forgot what quiet was like. What about you, you from around here?"

"Mostly."

"What's that mean"

"Born in Florida. Moved here when I was in third grade. Lived in Mobile when I was in junior high. Graduated high school and left for New York. Stayed there for a couple of years and then came back. The end."

"New York. I've been there a few times. But not to live."

"Some people love it. But I got tired and came back."

"You an actress?"

"I'm a sales clerk."

"I meant when you went up to New York."

"Student. I was going to school and so I just burned out on it all."

"I know the feeling. What were you studying?"

"Art. I was going to be an artist."

"What kind of art? Painting?"

"Sure. Oils and acrylics mostly. Sometimes watercolor, but oil was what I liked."

"Still paint?"

"No." Her eyes shifted down to her glass and then back to him. "I don't enjoy it any more."

"Sounds like that school was no damn good. What do you do now if you don't paint? Other than work at that store."

"I do a lot of sailing. It's good for me I think. Helps me relax. When I'm out on the bay there's no room for anything else. What do you do?"

"I'm afraid you got me there, darling'. I don't do much of anything but ride the bike."

"What would you be doing if you weren't here?"

"I'd probably be on the road to LA. I been getting the itch to go back."

"What's in LA?"

"Lights and noise. I'm a junkie for confusion."

"Not small town stuff."

"I grew up in small town stuff. Couldn't wait to get out of it."

"What about now? You seem like you're doing ok here."

"Yeah." He looked around him. "This isn't bad."

"When are you leaving?"

"A couple of days. Maybe. They're waiting on a part for my bike. That's the problem with a bike like mine. It's old."

"You should come down to the bay tomorrow and go sailing with me. Ever been on a boat?"

"A boat but no sailboat. What kind do you have?"

"It's just a 12 footer. Something I can handle by myself."

"I don't know anything about sailing."

"That's ok. All you got to do is what I tell you."

"I never been one to do what somebody told me. Not easy anyway. In your case though I wouldn't mind."

"On the boat always do what the captain says. Or she might make you walk the plank.

"I'll have to remember that. I'd hate to go swimming unexpected like."

Susan stood up, "I have to go. If you want to go sailing I'll be putting out about 8 tomorrow morning."

"Sounds good."

"Come on over to the marina. My boat is in slip 12. I'll keep an eye out for you."

"Aye, captain." He saluted.

"That's right. You learn quick." And she went back to the bar, picked up her purse, waved to her friends, and walked out the front door.

Jim Goings stood on the dock at 8 AM and watched the rain drive itself in sheets across the bay. The girl stepped off the dock and into the boat, "You ready?"

"You sail in rain?"

"Sure. It's just water. Wet's wet."

"You don't worry about lightening."

"Sometimes but not today. I checked the radar. Its just rain today." She slipped the tiller into its bracket on the transom. "Let's get going before the bay gets too choppy. "

Jim stepped into the boat gripping the gunwale as he edged his way down onto the seat.

"What's too choppy?"

"Untie that line up there and push us out."

"Aye captain." He reached over, rolling the boat as he pulled the line loose from the mooring and shoved them away from the slip. The waves slapped the boat as she maneuvered them out into the bay and the wind cracked the small sail in blasts of rain and invisible fists of air. The wind took the sail and heeled the boat to starboard.

Jim slipped down to sit in the slosh of water at the bottom of the boat.

He shouted at her, "You're crazy. You know that."

She smiled a split second before telling him to stay down and hang on. They didn't talk after that while she worked the tiller and the boom, moving them out into the bay, catching the wind steady and riding crest to crest, edging tiller and boom so that the sail balanced on the edge of luff and snap, careful not to wallow in the trough of any set of waves.

Jim watched her work. Her eyes watched only the shapes of waves and didn't see him.

He spent the two hours bailing water and sitting low in the boat. When she said to move to one side or the other, he did it without asking why. Other than her instructions, they did not talk. The boat caught the wind and angled across the face of the waves, not so far from shore he couldn't swim for it if he had to, but Susan guided it deftly from crest to crest, the only time she made him nervous was when she let the sail luff and the crack of the back edge worried him. She laughed at him each time he snapped his head around but the crack was not a gunshot. A pistol crack was not something he was comfortable hearing. Better to stay edgy and breathing.

"Sorry," she shouted into the wind. "I should have warned you."

"That's ok. Long as you know what you're doing."

"I do." And that was all they said until the squall died out and left them wallowing through choppy water.

"What made you want go to L.A.," she asked.

"What made you want to go to New York?"

"I already told you. I was going to be an artist. And to get out of here. But you haven't said how you ended up in L.A."

'Well that's a long story." He turned his face to the Mobile side of the bay.

The wind was dying fast and the rain was turned to mist. He draped his arm along the gunwale while he let the conversation die. Susan guided them south along the shore, jibing in front of the wind. Easing waves slapped the bow as they cut across the chop.

He reached into his shirt pocket for his pack of Picayunes but felt them wet and left them.

"It wasn't what I intended to do. It just turned out that way. When I was young I was a hell raiser. No interest in school. Drove my folks crazy so one day I got tired of that shit, got on my bike and took off. I was 17 and loose. Headed down to Mexico. Then I wandered around a bit doing stupid shit. Wonder I'm still alive."

Susan brought the boat about and tacked back toward Mobile. "You ever go home after that?"

"No. Too much time's gone by for that. After awhile we're all different people. You know?"

She didn't say anything.

A line of pelicans glided down the shoreline. He watched them slide in and out of line; a squadron, big birds. B24 bombers making a run on Romanian oil fields, Uncle Wallace told that story so many times it felt real. The pelican contours made him think of that, a squadron of B24s. They were big enough.

"I had a Russian friend in L.A. that would have liked sailing in this boat. He talked a lot about sailing on a lake in Russia when he was growing up, somewhere around St. Petersburg. That's where he was from. Alex would have liked this. He was a wild man. I think you would have liked him. He was very funny. Always telling jokes. Hard to understand him though. I never got used to the accent, after all those years, too. Didn't have the heart to tell him, so I just laughed like hell when he got to the punch line. I think he's probably been the best friend I had."

"Is he still in L.A.?"

"That's where he got buried."

"oh. Sorry."

"That's ok. It happens. The Russians are tough. That's one of the reasons I moved on. Started thinking I might not make it out of there alive. So one morning I told Alex I was heading east and turned my bike toward Houston. Before I hooked up with the Russians I used to ride out of Houston."

"They let you ride off like that?"

He pulled the cigarette lighter out of his pocket and rubbed it.

"Hard to give up the cigarettes."

"I imagine it is. How many packs a day?"

"I don't count em. Generally by now I'd be moving on to my second pack only this morning I never really got much of a start on the first one. It's pretty well soaked now."

"You ok?"

"Sure. I'm fine. Just got to do something with my fingers."

"What happened to Alex?"

"I wasn't there so only thing I know is from a guy riding out of L.A. Told me that Sergey, he was one of the Russians, wanted Alex' action. What the guy heard was after Sergey killed him, he had chopped off Alex's fingers and was hacking up the rest of him when the cops walked in the room. Said Sergey was busy flushing bits of Alex down the shitter when they showed up." He flipped the cover on the lighter open and closed open and closed. "Cops were looking to write a parking ticket when they stumbled into that mess. Sergey had driven up over the curb and stopped halfway on the sidewalk when he was running Alex down. Just like cops. Alex deserved better than that." He slipped the lighter back in his pocket. "Maybe we all do."

"Sounds like a crazy movie."

"Sometimes there's not much difference between crazy movies and what happens in real life."

"Guess so."

"Sometimes I think it's all just a dream. I feel better when I think about it like that. Anyway, I think Alex would have liked sailing out here on this water."

***

Jim spent the afternoon in a tourist bar. Susan was working until 5. He flexed his hands and watched the snakeheads move. Some of the girls at the bar asked if it was ok to touch them, like they were real snakes or something. Sure, he said, and they reached out an index finger to touch the scales. He told them that a guy in Monterey, California did them a long time ago. He was a real artist. The girls said, Oh, California, and nodded their heads. California explained many things for him without having to give any details. He didn't have to talk about hooking up with Alex in L.A., or Alex getting killed, or riding with the Lobos. None of those things meant anything here. None of them mattered. Nobody cared about any of that in Fairhope. He was just Jim, the guy with the snake tattoos who was getting his motorcycle fixed.

He watched the clock waiting for 5 and drank another beer.

***

Thursday afternoon he was sitting in The Pub having a drink with a girl named Nancy when his cell went off. It was the guy at the shop, "Your bike's ready."

"Great," he said.

"Sorry it took so long to get the parts."

"Sure, no problem."

"You want Roger to swing by and get you now?"

They wanted his money. Probably had to pay the bills for the week. He didn't blame them.

Jim looked outside. It was another nice day. "Sure, I guess. I'm over at The Pub."

"Thirty minutes."

He popped the cell back on the belt clip and told Nancy, "That was the shop. They got my bike ready."

Nancy smiled and said that was nice. "Are you going to leave?"

He didn't say anything. He shrugged and sipped his beer. He had thirty minutes before he had to go outside. He asked her, "Do you go to college here?"

She laughed and he watched her lips reveal her white teeth and she tilted her head back so that her hair spilled down her back and the sound flowed from her throat like music and he watched her for as long as he could.

***

A Ford 4x4 with a suspension lift passed, made a u-turn at the light, and came back to him, "Hey buddy, you the one that needs a ride to the shop?"

"You got it."

"Name's Roger. Climb on in."

"Good to meet you, Roger. I'm Jim."

"They said you had a little trouble with the bike."

"Broken drive belt."

"That's a bitch. You ain't going nowhere with one of those. Where were you headed?"

"I don't know, New Orleans, maybe."

"Nice town. I been there a few times. Do the clubs, hit the casinos. Course we got our share of those on the coast. But we don't have anything like Bourbon Street."

"That's a wild street."

"You from there?"

"No. A little town north of there, St. Helena. I grew up in St. Helena. But most of my life I lived other places." Outside the window, the houses and trees slid past. "What about you, where're you from?"

"I'm from Michigan. Moved down here about six years ago."

"Michigan. What the hell are you doing in Alabama?"

"Tired of the snow. I can ride my bike damn near year round down here."

"Gets kind of wet though."

"Sometimes but it ain't snow. Besides it don't get no better'n this."

"You don't sound like you're from Michigan."

"That's what some folks say. Here it is." Roger pulled the truck into the parking lot.

"You're a lucky man, Roger." Jim got out and walked into Retro Cycles.

Jim sat on the bike wearing his Key West shirt and shorts, Teva sandals. After three days in a Shady Brady, his Skid Lid felt out of place. He turned the key and thumbed the starter switch. The motor fired, thumping the air, and the guys from the shop stood outside to hear the engine sound. He cranked the throttle for them a couple of times, gave them a thumbs up for the good work, eased the clutch out, pulled onto the highway, made a u-turn a block down the road, and headed back to town, shirt whipping in the wind. In front of the shop, he redlined the engine at the shift point for third and held his fist high to the guys at the shop while he screamed the lyrics of Zevon's *My Ride's Here* to nobody.

He leaned back in the saddle after a few hundred feet of that. He had nowhere to go, nowhere that he had to be. Maybe he would head on back to New Orleans. Sounded like a plan.

Or Galveston would be better, down on the island to that little motel he holed up in last winter when things slowed down. Maybe Susan would want to go. Maybe he could talk her into painting again. She could paint pictures of seagulls and sail her boat.

He stopped at Blarney's and ordered a Turbo Dog with chips and salsa. Susan wasn't there yet. Surfside would be a good place to sit on the beach for a few weeks. Watch the waves eat away the land. That would be a good day.

He ordered another beer and waited. He was too old for this shit anymore.

Hydroformed

- Cocobolo -

Funeral Supper

After the man's funeral ended and his relatives returned to their homes, his sons, Edward and James, sat at the dining table with their mother. The house was silent except for the hollow knock of a clock in the living room and the occasional clatter of a spoon or knife on the mother's dishes.

James, that's what his family called him, reached across the table for the bowl of creamed potatoes.

His mother stared at the backs of his hands and said, "Your Daddy wouldn't have approved of those tattoos."

JB put the bowl by his plate and spooned out a mound of potatoes. "There's a lot about me he didn't approve of."

His mother poked at the green beans on her plate, moving them to the side, lined up evenly in small rows. "You never gave him a chance." Abruptly, she picked up her plate and went into the kitchen.

The brothers looked at each other, shrugged, but didn't say anything. They could hear her scraping plates and bowls, rinsing dishes, and covering casseroles.

They ate the rest of the potatoes and roast beef while they listened to her load the bowls and platters of left over food into her refrigerator.

JB dug his cigarettes and the old Zippo lighter out of his pockets and flipped the chromed cover open. "The old man was an ass," he said so that only Eddy could hear him.

"Don't you smoke in my house," his mother yelled from the kitchen.

JB snapped the cover closed and set the lighter and pack of cigarettes on the table by his plate. His mother turned the dishwasher on and left the kitchen. She walked through the dining room and living room on her way to her bedroom. She said nothing to them.

Eddy pushed back from the table. "I bought Angelo's a couple of months ago. Remember Angelo's?"

"Yeah. I remember. Why'd you buy that dump?"

"It was for sale."

"That's no reason." JB flexed his arms and stood up. "I got to take me a smoke break."

"Com'on down to Angelo's with me. You'll get a kick out of being down there again."

"Not in the life now, bro. Thanks though." JB opened the back door and went down the steps into the backyard. Eddy followed him out of the house.

It was a deep backyard with old water oaks growing along the back property lines. Tucked in a back corner was an empty kennel. They were as tall as ever; smooth barked gray trunks and long limbs. The oaks cast a high green cover over the perimeter and threw long lace shadows across the grass as the sun moved west and low.

The brothers walked out to the center of the backyard, St Augustine green under their shoes. Daylily beds oddly placed in bits of semicircle broke up the expanse. A white painted cast iron park bench was off to one side in the shade of a tree. JB swept his cigarette in an arc across the yard in front of them, "She never could figure out what to do with this yard."

"Old man wouldn't let her mess up his space."

JB walked the perimeter of the yard, stopping at a clump of early blooming camellias in the back corner.

"Damn Ed. These things are still here."

"I think almost everything survived."

"Almost." JB flicked the cigarette butt at the camellias.

"Why don't we get out of here and go down to Angelo's. Just a few minutes. I have the Camaro down there."

"Damn. Where'd you find it?"

"In the garage here."

"No shit."

"The old man had it under a cover."

"Does it run?"

"Sure. I tuned it up and changed the oil. That's all it took. Cranked right up."

"No shit." JB walked to the bench and sat down, stretched his legs out, planting the heels of his boots on the hard clay. Where it wasn't covered in grass, the yard showed sandy river clay, gray and tight, hard as rock when it was dry and not much softer when it was wet.

Eddy sat beside him. "You remember the time the old man bought those live pheasants?"

"Damn I forgot all about that. Had 'em stuffed in the trunk of the car. Why was it they got live pheasants anyway? I don't remember that part."

"Momma got a crazy idea to fix pheasant for dinner one weekend. I think she got the idea from a TV cooking show."

"Lucky they had their wings clipped."

"Hada helluva time running those things down as it was."

"Don't blame them for running."

"I guess they caught them all."

"As I recall. I don't remember the details other than the birds exploding out of the trunk when the old man lifted the lid."

"That was pretty good seeing him standing there in front of the trunk grabbing after that bunch of screaming feathers going in all directions all around him."

JB dug his cigarettes and the old Zippo lighter out of his pockets and flipped the chromed cover open. "The old man was an ass," he said and lit another cigarette.

"Where do you live now?"

"Nowhere." JB pressed the cigarette butt into the cold iron arm of the bench before flipping it out into the yard. "I stay on the road most of the time." He lit another. "Met this girl over in Alabama a few months ago but that didn't work out. Been thinking of going back to L.A. I got some friends out there I haven't seen in a couple of years."

"I have an apartment down in Hammond. You could stay there for a while if you want. It's a two bedroom."

"I'm better off on my own. You know?"

They sat on the bench listening to the wind move above them, high in the trees, splitting itself between the leaves, dividing and merging and churning.

"Got my start running shit out of Angelo's." JB squinted into a shaft of sunlight that slipped through the green canopy. "Driving that damn Camaro all over hell and gone. That was some crazy shit back then."

"Why don't you come on down to the place. Just to take a look."

"Don't think so, little bro."

"I got Julie working down there. Hannah's in the fifth grade."

JB looked at his brother. "That's another reason not to go down there. Why didn't you buy something worth having? Like a Quicky Mart, or something. You could make some money around here with one of those."

"I do ok with the bar. Don't get held up either. Not like any Quicky Mart."

"Yeah. Guess not. Not Angelo's." JB stood up. "It's getting cold. Why don't we go on inside. Maybe there's a football game on or something."

"I think Georgia is on cable. They're playing Florida tonight."

Eddy followed his brother into the house, talking about the chances that Georgia had to win the national championship. JB let him talk. Florida was a 14-point favorite. In the house, JB pulled a couple of brews out of the refrigerator and sat on the sofa in front of the TV. The old man bought cheap beer but it was better than nothing. JB popped the tops and put the beers on the coffee table.

Eddy dug a bag of chips out of the pantry. "You want dips or salsa?"

JB shouted, "Salsa, man. I ain't from New York City," and they laughed. It was an old joke in the family.

Eddy brought the chips and salsa to the den. "You ain't changed much."

"Here's your beer." JB leaned over and handed Eddy a can. "You know where the old man kept the remote?"

"In his chair. I got it." Eddy pulled the remote from under a cushion and turned the set on. "Dad hated the Gators."

They sat back on the sofa, sipping beer and eating chips with salsa. Eddy said, "Pretty funny huh. Watching the Gators today."

"Yeah. He'd die if he knew," and they roared, He'd die if he knew, over and over in waves of sound on sound, at the edge of crazy but not quite over the line.

"What's so funny." Their mother stood in the doorway, hands on her hips.

"Nothing, mom," Eddy said. "We were just thinking how Dad never liked the Gators and that's the only game on TV this afternoon."

"That's not funny." She walked past them into the kitchen.

"Sure you don't want to go down to Angelo's?" Eddy motioned over his shoulder to the kitchen where their mother was putting away pots and pans, banging aluminum on aluminum. "We could watch the game down there. Drink some good beer."

"This is fine." JB grinned at Eddy. "It's good being home for a change."

"Liar."

They laughed together. JB raised his beer can in a mock salute. "Maybe so, little bro. Maybe so."

They watched the game, shouting when Georgia kicked a field goal, shouting when Florida scored a touchdown. They were home again for a little while. Florida kicked Georgia's ass.

Their mother sat at the dining room table with a cup of coffee and a small plate with a slice of chocolate cake. She let them make noise while they watched the game. It wasn't a sound that stayed with her. The sound that stayed with her was the echo of the man closing his truck door. The echo of the man calling his bird dog across the yard stayed with her. The opening and closing of doors as the man moved through the house, in and out of the house, those echoes would not leave. She sipped coffee and ate a bite of chocolate cake.

The man was gone but his echo filled her house.

Outside of the bay window, the light faded as the sun dropped low. Fall afternoons ended so quickly. She held her cup in her hands, pooled her fingers around it, let the heat warm the ice out of her skin. She bowed her head over it and sighed. In the den, the boys yelled about something in the football game. They had come home too late to change the way life ended for the man. There had been no laughter for him in the house.

With her tongue she pressed the chocolate cake against the roof of her mouth, pressed it into a smooth paste. Waited for the taste. Waited for the dusky flavor of chocolate to touch her tongue. It was paste, tasteless, flavorless. She swallowed and it was a lump in her throat. She sipped coffee and moved it down into her gut. A lump of chocolate paste...that was life she said.

She sat at the dining room table and watched the outside become night while the boys whooped it up in the den over a football game.

Eddy left the house after the 10 o'clock news. He said he wasn't going to the bar tonight. He had gotten somebody named Errol to take it. He was just going back to his apartment to get some sleep. He leaned over so that she could kiss him on the cheek and then he was gone. She heard his motorcycle start and then he was gone, leaving behind a whining engine snarl that grated on her nerves.

"James, are you planning on staying here tonight?"

"I was thinking that I might."

"You can stay in your old room. The sheets on the bed are fresh." She looked around her feet, "You have any luggage?"

"I got a bag on the bike." He stepped outside and returned in minute with a black leather saddlebag slung over his shoulder.

"Is that what you carry your clothes in?"

"I travel light."

She walked down the hall to her bedroom. "If you need anything, the towels are in the hall closet. I don't think you'll need any extra blankets tonight." She went in her room. "Let me know if you can't find anything."

"I will."

She closed her door.

He flipped on the light in his old room. The walls were painted pale blue and the carpet was gold. All of it was new. The old graffiti was lost. The stains in the old carpet were gone. He tossed the bag across the bed and pulled out his travel kit. In this house, he wouldn't need it. His mother kept extras of everything in the guest bathroom. That used to be his bathroom, his and Eddy's.

His opened the bathroom door, curious to see what she had changed in there. It had a fake marble sink now, a pale yellow composite with white swirls. Faded blue vinyl wallpaper that had yellow flowers in it covered the walls. It was nothing like the maroon tile bathroom sink and white sheetrock walls they had when he was a kid. This was his mother's mind. All trace of his life erased from the house.

JB finished his shower. He didn't know they still made Prell shampoo. Dial soap in the shower. She still bought the same stuff. Pepsodent toothpaste, the Sunflower Store must not have changed their stock in 30 years. At least this much was still the same.

He settled into the bed, the sheets stiff and clean, cold at first slowly warmed. The smell of the room had changed. It was some sort of potpourri. She probably made it herself. At Christmas she used to like to do those oranges with cloves stuck in them.

He closed his eyes. Maybe he'd go over to Angelo's tomorrow. See what Eddy was doing. Maybe see Julie. He'd spent more time at Angelo's than here. After that he'd hit the road. Go back to L.A. or somewhere new. He opened his eyes and stared at the fluorescent stars still stuck on the ceiling. He couldn't think of anywhere new to go.

- Cocobolo -

ParvAneh

Melissa Vicknair was working in the stacks at NeuFiels Books, restocking shelves and restoring order in the stacks. She enjoyed the boredom of it, the repetitive actions her hands could perform while her mind traveled. Sometimes the jacket of a new book would spark a train of thought that carried her to Europe or Asia. Her favorite places to mind travel were in ancient Asia, along the silk route, in the highest deserts of the world, and through mountain passes in the Himalayas.

She was certain that the true Garden of Eden was in eastern Afghanistan. She saw it as a secret valley hidden in the highest mountains on a forgotten ancient trade route and she would go there, someday, to the place and people that she believed she loved. But that was a lie she told herself because she knew that she would always be an American and was certain that by simply being in a spot she would change it so that it was not what it was, and she could not see it as it was. Besides, she was also convinced the Afghans would kill her on sight if she went. She was sad about that.

She slid another misplaced book in its proper location.

She had just murmured, "Why couldn't people get these things right? Didn't they know the alphabet?" when she heard the sound of "Hi, M." from behind her. She flinched at being called M inside her sanctuary. The hated abbreviation of her name concocted by Allie, but it wasn't Allie, it was a man's voice. She saw the dark haired guy from Allie's party standing between the rows of books on shelves.

"Remember me?"

"You were at Allie's party." At the party, she had mind-named him Rasputin since he made her think of the monk. She didn't remember his real name.

"Yeah, that's me. So, what are you doing here?"

She didn't want to tell him, "I work here." However, there was no time to devise a plausible lie and she would just have to work it out somehow if things turned awkward for some reason, like he was insane or something. So, she told him that she did in fact work in the bookstore.

Standing in the aisle holding a copy of her book he scanned the volumes around him. "Seems to fit you."

She wasn't sure how to take that, good or bad, and said, "Are you going to buy my book?"

He looked at the book in his hand. "I thought it was interesting."

"I can sign it for you if you want."

"Ok. That would be good. How about some coffee when you get a break? You can sign it then."

She never took her breaks but said she would meet him at the coffee shop across the street in 30 minutes. That was the best she could do. She said that apologetically to be polite but hoped he wouldn't want to wait around for half an hour.

He told her that sounded good, took the book, and checked out.

***

Rasputin was sitting at a table when she arrived. He motioned to her as she walked into the coffee shop and she responded with a half wave, discreetly shoulder high on her walk to the counter. She ordered a large cup of Garuda blend.

"Sorry about the other night," he said as she sat in the bistro chair. "It must have been difficult having a parade of strangers in your room."

"That's Allie," she said and sipped her coffee so that she didn't have to say anything more.

"I suppose." He offered a plate of chocolate dipped biscotti. "Would you like a biscotti?"

"Thanks," she took one and dipped it in her Garuda. "I always think of buying some but never do. Usually I just pick up a cup of coffee and go back to the store. So, how is it you know Allie?"

"I met her at the gallery. She was setting up a show and I was trying to get the financials straightened out."

"I'd have never guessed. I expected you were an artist or musician. Musician I guess. You don't look like an accountant."

"It's not something I do full time anymore. What sort of musician?"

"That's hard. Classical I think. French horn."

"Why not jazz?"

"I don't know. Maybe you look more measured than I'd think a jazz musician would be. I'd expect their tempo to be somewhere at an extreme.

"Why French horn and not bassoon or tympani?"

"Bassoon is a reed instrument and you don't seem that restrained to me. I think of you as more of a horn instrument person, but not loud, not a coronet. And the tympani doesn't suit your personality. So I think you're more of a French horn."

"I'm no musician."

"So it doesn't matter. What do you do full time?"

"I trim trees."

She stared at him. "To what extent? Do you mean around your house or professionally?"

He laughed. He had a big laugh and she was embarrassed by it in the coffee shop.

"I'm an arborist."

"I don't think I've known anyone that did that, other than gardening stuff. Going out with a lopper or a saw and whacking away on a limb. Did you go to school for that or did you just pick it up?"

"I went to school. An arborist is more like a vet than a gardener. To get your certification you have to study the tree, mulch, fertilizers, and pests. It's not just pruning." He stared at her while he sipped his coffee. "Although that's important. "

"I never thought about it before."

"The worst thing is seeing the trees that people mutilate. They're living beings you know. The trees that is."

"Right." She nibbled on the biscotti and wondered if he was nuts or serious. He knew where she lived, where she worked. He had been in her room, seen her things. He made her nervous. She finished the biscotti. "You're an accountant and an arborist. How'd that happen?"

"Please, I can't eat all of these." He slid the plate of biscotti closer to her and she hesitated but took another.

"How did you end up being an arborist full time and not an accountant? Seems like you'd do better as an accountant."

"I do alright and I like working with trees. So, have you decided what your next book will be about?"

She dipped the biscotti into her Garuda and bit off the end of it. He sat across from her watching her over the rim of his cup as he sipped coffee and waited for her to say.

"It's about an ancient legend from the middle east. Not really a historical novel since it's not history. More of a retelling of the legend."

"Which legend?"

"It's hard to describe." She wasn't sure that she wanted to tell him. It was bad luck to tell a story before it was written. Whenever she did, she lost the edge of the piece. "I ran across it when I was doing research on my novel."

"When do you think you'll be finished?"

"I don't know. I'm just starting on it. Here," she reached out for the copy of her novel, "let me sign this for you before I forget."

Rasputin handed her the book and she opened the cover, "What should I say?"

"To my good friend Jeffry. That sounds ok."

"How do you spell Jeffery?" He didn't look like a Jeffery. "Or would you rather Jeff?" She always pictured Jefferies as blond headed surfers, extras in old beach party movies.

"J-e-f-f-r-y. I don't care for Jeff. It sounds like a peanut butter label."

She handed the book back to him, now inscribed to her good friend Jeffry. "Allie is the only one that calls me M. I don't know why she does. I don't really like it. It sounds like half of a candy. Everyone else calls me Melissa. So, are you from San Francisco?"

"I moved up from southern California a few years ago. I don't usually tell people here. They hate L.A. so I don't say. Don't tell anyone, ok?"

"Yeah." She shrugged. She wouldn't be talking about him to anyone anyway so it didn't matter.

"How about you. How long have you lived here?"

She dipped her biscotti into the coffee again before she told him that she moved out to go to college. She wasn't comfortable with his knowing details. He already knew more than he needed to as far as she was concerned. "I have to get back. I've been gone too long."

"Sure." He slipped the remaining biscotti into a paper bag and stood up with her. "I have to get going myself. There's a place over on Jackson that I have to do this afternoon. Nothing spectacular. Just cleanup. I'm shaping this young tree so that it won't have to be topped." He followed her out of the shop. "Most people just plant a tree because they like the way it looks in a park or a magazine. They never consider what it's going to become in ten or twenty years. This tree I'm working with is a black pine so it has potential. One of my clients had planted redwoods next to a power line." Jeffry crossed the street with her. "I had to remove them. That was sad. You can't shape redwoods. People end up topping them when they're like that. They might as well remove them. The tree is never going to recover from that. It's sort of a life at any price approach to things. I hate that. You know what I mean?"

He stopped walking and stared at her face.

She said, "Sure," but she really didn't understand what he was talking about. The words spilled out of him too fast. She kept walking. She just wanted to get back inside the store and finish straightening the stacks.

He kept pace with her.

"I was born in Alabama," he said. "I don't usually tell anybody but Allie said you were from the south too."

"Louisiana."

"Around here if you say you're from Alabama they look at you like you're a freak so I don't say. It keeps things normal."

"I never noticed." She reached for the door.

"You're from Louisiana. That's different." He stopped and stood holding his book and bag. "Well, I guess we're here."

"Yes." She reached for the door. "Thanks for the biscotti. I hope you enjoy the book."

"I'm sure I will. I know the author." He smiled at her but she was stepping into the store and didn't notice.

As she crossed the threshold, she turned for a moment and made a half wave to him before she let the door close behind her. He hesitated and then crossed the street, disappearing between the cars and was gone. She dropped her empty coffee cup into the wastebasket behind the counter and returned to the stacks where she resumed restoring order to their momentary chaos while planning the opening of her new piece, *ParvAneh, an ancient legend of the Silk Road by M. Vicknair*

In an ancient time, before the waging war of Alexander, before the Europeans, a proud people came out of the steppes and down through the mountain passes into what is now known in the west as northeastern Afghanistan. They were called the Hz by the few who lived in that region because they were travelers from across the mountain ranges. Their women wore silks covered in golden leaf that shimmered in the breezes of the high mountains and their men wore leathers, fleece, and furs that shielded them from the mountain cold. The people laughed with large smiles and white teeth, singing and playing music as they traveled. With them, they drove their flocks of sheep and goats careful to protect them from the snow leopards and grey wolves that prowled the edges of their journey. When the people reached the high deserts of the ancient trail that connected the peoples of the Orient to the peoples of Asia they paused in a fertile valley sheltered from the bitterest wind and carpeted in green growing grass, enough to feed their flocks and more. It was a good place and the people made their home there, tired of traveling and they were happy.

.

***

Melissa went through her afternoon routine of working the sales counters, updating the inventory lists, packaging book orders, and boxing unsold stock. Each day varied in the duration of individual tasks but each day required the same tasks and to that extent, she could measure time.

During the late hours of work, she told Barbra who worked in the New Age section about Rasputin. She said she liked that name for him better than Jeffry. And she didn't trust him. He seemed to know too much about her.

Barbra said that she shouldn't turn everything into literature and sometimes coffees and biscotti were just things humans consumed. Perhaps the Universe brought Rasputin to the bookstore. It was karma. She shouldn't worry. The Universe would take care of her.

When Barbra said that, Melissa frowned. She didn't focus on metaphysical rationale for the motion of atomic clouds. At NeuFiels, that was difficult not to do. But she liked her routine and resolved to smile at Barbra and thank her for her advice. This was also part of her daily routine.

Barbra wanted to know if he was cute and Melissa said, if he was, she wouldn't have named him Rasputin.

Barbra told her that she thought he sounded mysterious, an old soul trapped in this plane unable to move forward. Perhaps it was Melisa's purpose to serve as a guide for his transcendence from this level to the next.

Melissa couldn't resist saying, "Guns, knives, or poison?"

Barbra didn't joke about the cosmos. She was old, a real hippie left over. She still wore tie-dyed dresses and blouses. She believed a cosmic wheel drove events in obscure patterns. Barbra stopped talking and left the stacks. That was how Barbra worked, like a shaking can of cola in the sun. One time, Eloisa, who used to work in the Travel section, made a comment about Barbra's hair. Barbra had worn a flower in it one day for some reason, and Eloisa told her it looked a bit tired. After two weeks of silence, Barbra threw a piece of roll at Eloisa during lunch and called her a selfish troll. Barbra called her a troll until Eloisa cried and left the store. Wacky drama like that didn't happen often so when it did it stuck out of the regular monotony like a boulder on a beach. Melissa would apologize for the joke. Better that than have Barbra explode next week.

Melissa wandered back to the astrology section where Barbra was working and told her that she was only trying to make a joke because she was anxious about the Rasputin guy. That Barbra was right, he probably was there for a reason. She would stay open to the universe; wait to see if there was something that she should do.

Barbra told her, "That's ok. Everything happens for a reason you know. Sometimes we just don't understand it yet. But it will all be ok. Everything becomes clear in time. You'll see."

Melissa wanted to puke but held it down and went back to the front counter satisfied that Barbra would be ok. Monotony would stay in the store and there would be no drama that day or next week. She shouldn't have said anything about Rasputin. Never again.

***

Melissa took the cable car to Market and switched to the bus to make the final leg down Haight. Her agent wanted to meet at a coffee shop on Cole and go over changes to her Dutch Bayou draft. Melisa liked the shop and enjoyed the trip. It was a nice diversion and not too far off her routine path. The buildings were more intimate; the trees gave it shade and softened the lines of concrete curb and pavement. If she had to leave the house near Geary, this is where she would want to live.

She was early and the shop was almost empty at that time of the afternoon. Half way between lunch and dinner, she was able to get a table by the window and sat with her cappuccino and watched the street. There was a hardware store of some kind across the street and it seemed so out of place for San Francisco that she wondered what it was like inside. Mary, her agent, said that this used to be a real valley with dairy farms before it was city. Melissa tried to create an image of the street with only a few stores, the hardware store would be one and perhaps a few buildings around it, and then on the blocks back from that the small farms. She expected that they would be 20 or 40-acre places. Even without the houses, there wasn't much land in here to support more than that. And if the farms were larger there would be too few people to support the hardware store. She enjoyed the sensation of seeing the slopes in green grass and the street in dirt and mud with boardwalks to line its edges. She checked her watch. Mary was 10 minutes late. She ordered another cappuccino and began marking through sections of her manuscript while she waited.

> *In the valley, high in the cold mountains, the Hz made a city that spread along a mountain river and the road between east and west passed through its center. On the low slopes of the rolling land around the city, the grass was green and along the river edge, trees grew scattered across the land bearing fruit in their season, an oasis set in the midst of stone and sand.*

The sight of Rasputin crossing the street toward her snapped Melissa's imagery of Cole Valley as a pastoral setting, brought back the thundering blast of Metro busses and rumbling trucks and whining cars over cracked and patched asphalt. She had an impulse to race to the restroom and lock herself inside until he passed but that was crazy and she sat by the plate glass window and watched him walk closer. If he had seen her, and how could he have missed seeing her sitting by that wide wall of glass, that she was there alone, then he might be coming inside to sit and talk. It was too late to slip away to the counter and order another cappuccino, to fade back into the darker inside of the shop where he would not see her. If he did come inside, what then? She didn't know. Perhaps she would smile and say something about it being odd to see him over here. What was he doing over here? Perhaps he had followed her. He had turned up at the bookstore in a strange way pretending he didn't know she worked there. She questioned his motives. He knew she worked there. He must have. Allie probably told him. Here he was walking into the coffee shop.

Rasputin opened the door of the coffee shop and went to the counter, ordered a coffee and biscotti and sat at a table on the far side of the room reading a book. She could not see the title. He was too far away. It was awkward for her, not wanting to be bothered by him but resenting being snubbed. She sipped her cappuccino and watched out the window for Mary. She was 20 minutes late now. Perhaps it was the wrong day. Perhaps it was next week. She might have fallen and broken her leg or arm. She might be in the hospital.

Melissa reached into her daypack for the appointment book and verified that the meeting was today. The best thing to do was remain calm and wait. It was extra time to work on the manuscript. And she would ignore Rasputin sitting across the empty room with his book and coffee and biscotti. If he was still there after Mary had come and gone then she might say something to him. That would be the polite thing to do.

> *In a year before the long winter, a band of adventurers riding horses came down from the mountain passes into the valley. Among the band, a prince of the northlands traveled in disguise with his guardians. He was handsome on his dark horse, towering over those who walked and the chief's daughter, ParvAneh, noticed him as he and his guardians rode into her father's city.*

Melissa scribbled notes in the margin of her manuscript, clues for herself to puzzle over later about the characters, colors of dresses and silver decorations on bridles, the sound of bells that fell and rose as the prince's horse trotted on stony ground.

"I see you're busy working on the manuscript." It was Mary, arrived at last and sliding into the chair across from her, leather brief case laid flat on the table. Mary always laid her brief case on the table. She said it was so she would not forget it when she left. A nice case, thin with a flap that latched shut, Melissa had considered buying one for herself until she saw the price and decided to keep her day pack.

"It's not working. I don't like it." Melissa closed her manuscript and capped her pen.

"That's good. Best not to be too much in love with it. So, how're things at the house?"

"Ok. I moved my toaster down to the kitchen and fixed supper down there a few times last week."

"Did she say anything?""

"Not Allie. She was very helpful. Real nice about it."

"I see. Give me a moment I want to get a latte." Mary walked up to the counter and while she stepped across the wooden floor the hard tap of her spike heels caused Rasputin to glance up and Melissa could not ignore him without being too peculiar so she smiled at him and lifted her fingers in a hidden wave. He grinned at her and said "hello" to which she had to reply "hi" and then he asked if she were busy. Melissa pointed toward Mary who was waiting at the counter for her European sized cup of latte and said "my agent" to him. Rasputin nodded and gave her a thumbs up which didn't make sense to her but she decided it was supposed to be good luck or maybe he hoped her agent liked her manuscript. She wasn't sure but told him "thanks" and by that time Mary was walking back to the table with her over-large cup balanced on an over-large saucer.

"I just love this Buffalo china," Mary said as she settled once more onto the wooden chair. "My husband insists that we use it. The plain white that is. The sort you used to find in roadside cafes. I don't mind I suppose. It has such a solid feel to it."

"I almost bought some once at a garage sale."

"Why didn't you?"

"I didn't need it. No place to put it really."

"You have to call me if you ever find some more. The classic Buffalo china is just fantastic. What we have now is reproduction. Still good but not the same. I think it might be the weight of time as much as anything. Harold says that archeologists will be digging it up intact a thousand years from now. The only existent pieces of dinnerware to survive the asteroid."

"What asteroid?"

"That's just Harold. He uses that as his metaphor for the collapse of society by some unknown calamity. Harold is convinced that one can't predict these things. People are just going along like any other day and then for some reason things begin to stop working. His theory is that it's the little things that go first, the things few people notice until they cascade upwards to the big things and then society itself. Harold just loves that idea, the impermanence of everything. I prefer to enjoy the belief that this is all going to be here tomorrow whether it is or not. I don't need asteroids."

"But he thinks Buffalo china is permanent."

"To some extent I suppose he does. I'll have to tell him so."

The adventurers paused in the city to rest and procure supplies before following the road west, which was their stated quest, to travel to its end and the unknown lands. ParvAneh contrived to meet the prince and had her father invite the adventurers to a celebration of the harvest. While at the celebration the prince was introduced to ParvAneh and they spent the evening of the celebration in laughter and conversation. The prince, smitten by the beautiful ParvAneh, convinced his companions to remain with him in the city until spring when the road would clear of snow.

Mary sipped her latte and for a minute there was no talking and the two of them watched the people and the traffic outside the plate glass moving up and down Cole. The pause in conversation gained weight as it grew longer and with a sense of compulsion and regret Melissa spoke to break it before it consumed the meeting, "Did you have a chance to read my proposal?"

"I did." The spell was broken. "By the way, before I forget, here are my notes for your manuscript. I liked your characterization of the community. Dutch Bayou's not the sort of place one thinks of as Louisiana. But it has an odd sense of verisimilitude, a very authentic tone. What I'd like to know more of up front though is what is at stake for the protagonist in this piece. The narrative arc needs to be better defined. I'm thinking that the story actually begins at the third chapter. Read it and see what you think." Mary slid a manila envelope from her briefcase to Melissa who took it and placed it in her daypack.

"What about the proposal?"

Mary sipped her latte and glanced outside at a bus lumbering past. "It's an interesting idea but I'm not sure how to market it. Retelling lost legends. It's a bit obscure. The audience might be restricted. A few academic readers perhaps." She set her cup down with a hard clack into its saucer. "When you have a few chapters, I'll be happy to read them of course but I can't promise anything. Everything is so competitive right now. It's worse than ever. No one reads anymore."

In that interlude, the prince spent much time with the daughter of the chief and her court telling tales of adventures in lands outside the valley. The growing bond between the prince and ParvAneh angered Behrouz, the shaman of the tribe. Each day Behrouz watched the young prince and the chief's daughter spend time laughing and in quiet conversation. The shaman was an ambitious man who had determined to wed ParvAneh and then, through craft, deftly poison the chief as part of a scheme to become leader of the Hz. Behrouz resolved to kill the prince in a manner so subtle that none would suspect him as the originator of the tragic demise.

Melissa watched Rasputin sit at his table reading, holding the book with one hand, fingers forming a holder, while he sipped coffee and ate his biscotti with the other. Melissa watched him, his hands didn't look like a gardeners, he was pale, and except for the flannel shirts he looked like he should be sitting in an office somewhere. She didn't see him working outside. He was too thin, too frail.

"Harold wants to move to Mendocino."

"It's beautiful up there."

"I'm dying for a cigarette right now." Mary's fingers moved as though they felt the cigarette. "I haven't smoked in years but today I could start again."

"I never smoked."

"It's too damned expensive now. I don't see how kids can afford it."

"Right." She was surprised to hear Mary say kids. Saying it, she sounded old. Like her mother, her mother would say kids. "Why don't you want to move to Mendocino?"

"I like the city too much."

"It's not that far away."

"I don't want to have to make the drive. Harold says I should just quit and go up there and write. I used to write before this."

"Sounds wonderful."

"I'm not really an artist type. It's ok for a weekend away from the city, but to be up there day after day.... I think it might drive me crazy. What would I do?"

"Why does he want to move?'

"God knows." She finished her coffee and stood. "I have to go. I have someone coming by the house in a few minutes. Give me a call if you have any questions about my comments," and she was gone, a flurry of dark long coat, brief case, and scarf.

Melissa opened the envelope to see how many notes were stuck on the first page. Mary liked to use sticky notes for her comments, long comments, sometimes spilling across multiple sticky notes. Corrections and edits she wrote on the page but comments went on sticky notes. Melissa counted five of them on the first page, three on the second. Mary wrote essays on those notes, with attributions. Melissa didn't like to read them. They made her feel dull. She rushed through the first note and spotted a reference to Forrester and then Welty and on the second note McCarthy. She thought of categories in a TV game show that Allie watched at night.

"Hi Melissa."

Rasputin stood by the table, Melissa hadn't seen him cross the room and wasn't certain how long he had been standing there holding his cup, saucer, and dish of biscotti.

"Mind if I sit?"

"Go ahead. What are you doing over here?"

"I live up the street. A couple of blocks." He motioned out of the window toward the slope of hill covered in houses shielded by trees that rose behind the hardware store.

"It's bizarre seeing you in here."

"Twice in a week."

"Yeah. I had a meeting with my agent. She lives near here. I usually meet her here. It's better than going downtown...for her. It wouldn't matter for me. I come over here from the bookstore so I could just as easily go downtown." She stopped talking. The sound of her words annoyed her. Too fast, too tense, she stopped.

"It's a nice place. This time of the afternoon it's quiet but lunchtime it's a mad house. I never come in here at lunch."

"I've only been here in the afternoon."

"They make a good salad. It's a meal. No meat. Chick peas and toasted sesame seeds, baby spinach, arugula, if you get a chance to try it some time check it out."

"Maybe I will."

"Want a biscotti?" He nudged the dish toward her and she picked one. It was drizzled in chocolate.

"Thanks." and dipped it into the last of her coffee. It melted on her tongue in dusky almond chocolate flavors. Rasputin wasn't the right name for him. She would have to think of another.

*ParvAneh and the prince fell ill after eating their evening meal. Immediately the shaman was called. When he arrived and saw that ParvAneh had been poisoned with the prince, his face paled and his hands grew restless, tugging at his mustache and **pressing** smooth the silk of his robe against his chest. Muttering curses, Behrouz the shaman left the room and rushed to collect his herbs. Returning with bowls and potions, Behrouz began his magic incantations and mixing* *of potions seeking a remedy for his ill-conceived subterfuge.*

"Do you always have biscotti with your coffee?"

"Not really but it seems like it, doesn't it. I suppose I do if I'm out, but not at home. Not usually."

"What kind?"

"I like the almond. What do you like?"

"Chocolate is ok. This is good. I'm always fascinated how hard it is before dipping it in coffee. You could break a tooth on it."

"Do you like biscotti?"

"I suppose. I don't have it often enough to have an opinion."

"We should have coffee more often then so you can develop one. I tried making it once but it didn't turn out. It was just better buying it at the coffee shop."

"Did your mother make it? When you were growing up?"

"No, not her. She doesn't cook. We lived on microwave food. Plastic bags of already cooked stuff."

"The way you say it that doesn't sound very good. My momma always cooked for us. She used to say microwaves were for lazybones."

He drank some coffee and watched an old man push on the pedestrian button. The old man was pushing it over and over and over trying to make it change. "She wasn't lazy. She just didn't want to cook. See that old man over there pushing the button."

She glanced out where he was pointing and saw the man stooped and relentlessly pressing the button.

"He reminds me of a pigeon in a Skinner box."

"What's a Skinner box?"

"This guy named B.F. Skinner made this box that you could put an animal in, usually a pigeon. In the box are two buttons, white and black or round and square, different from each other so that when the bird pecked the right button some corn or seeds would fall down into a bowl. That was their reward. Look there he goes. The light finally changed."

The old man scurried across the street staying in the middle of the pedestrian striped walkway.

"Next time he gets up there he'll push that button again until the light changes."

"What if it doesn't?"

"Good question. I don't know." They sat at the table eating biscotti and sipping coffee while watching the crowds outside gather at the stoplight waiting for the pedestrian signal to change. After a minute, Rasputin said, "He might stand there pushing the button and not give up. That would be a good experiment. We could set up a camera here and record the entire thing. Like God was messing with him. He'd never know."

"Sounds cruel."

"Sure. But that's only if he kept pushing the button for no reason."

"You said you were from Alabama?"

"Mobile. Actually a town across the bay from Mobile."

"I was down there doing a reading. What town?

"A little place. Fairhope. It was an old utopian village started back in the early 1900s.

"That's where I was. How'd you end up out here?"

"My mom was from Santa Monica my dad was from Alabama. I moved out here when I graduated from high school. My folks split up about then and she moved out too."

"What about your dad."

"He stayed on the coast. Different little places near Mobile. Mostly eastern shore."

"My folks live up the river from New Orleans. I don't go back very often. What about you? You go see your dad any?"

"No. He stroked out a few years ago. But I see my mom for Christmas. She's still in Sana Monica. Easter, I go down there for that. She's real big on holidays and going to church so I humor her. I tell her she lived in Alabama too long. Because of the church stuff."

"You're' not religious."

"No. You?"

"Not me. But my folks are."

"Catholic?"

"Sure."

"Mom's a Baptist. I think I could deal with it if she was Methodist or Presbyterian. Don't know how she got to be Baptist."

"I don't believe in organized religion."

"Me either. There's a story about Skinner that one night he forgot to turn off the feeder in the box and the next day he came in and the birds were all in their boxes acting bizarre. Some of them were hitting their heads on the walls. Others were staggering around like they were drunk. Skinner freaked. Had no idea what was wrong with the birds, bad corn or something, maybe. Then he noticed the feeder was randomly churning out seeds. The birds were thinking that whatever they did when the seeds dropped out made it happen so they kept doing the same stupid things over and over until the seeds would drop. After an evening, they had developed elaborate rituals to make the seeds fall into the feed bowl. Of course it was just the dispenser motor running but stupid pigeons don't know like the stupid little old man down there. He thinks pressing that button makes the light change faster. I think that's what religion is."

"Your point is that God is Skinner?"

"Actually I was going for there not being a God but maybe Skinner is better. He was bizarre looking, big head sort of bald. Looked like an alien. That's god. The machine is just running."

"You're a cynic."

"I was thinking I was an existentialist."

"They're more optimistic than you. I don't think you have any leap of faith. Just the anxt."

"Leap of faith makes me think of Half Dome. I was up at Yosemite last week. You ever been up there?"

"I don't travel much. No car. "

"You should go sometime, even if you have to hitch. It's amazing. The air has a quality to it. San Francisco is better than L.A. but nothing like the Sierras. If I could live up there I would."

"Lots of trees. Right?"

He laughed and Melissa watched him. He looked odd when he laughed, mouth crooked, twisted up at the left corner, uncomfortable. She didn't recall his laugh at the party. His face did not easily adopt the shape, more tormented than tormentor.

He was Basil Rathbone in Sherlock Holmes, without an accent. He didn't sound like he was from Alabama. He sounded more mid-western. "What's your most favorite thing about Yosemite?"

"That's tough."

"I've seen Ansel Adams photos. I think I would like the waterfalls best."

"They're good. The hike to Half Dome is something else though. You won't see the view from up there in many photos. I should take you up there sometime. You'd never forget it."

"I don't think so."

"It's just a thought. Don't say no so fast."

"I'm not really an outside person." She checked her watch. "I have to go. I have a lot of work to do tonight."

"Maybe we could have coffee again sometime."

She picked up her daypack and papers. "Sure, why not."

"How often are you over here?"

"Not often. When I need to meet with Mary, that's about it."

"I could come by the bookstore then. How about next Tuesday? I'll be over working on a couple of Japanese maples."

"Maybe. Got to go," and Melissa ran out the door for the bus stop, leaving him cradling his oversized cup of coffee in the palms of his hands while he watched her. From his seat at the window, he could see her cross the street to the stop and in a blur the bus passed through the intersection stopped and pulled away, and like magic, she had disappeared.

Majeed, the prince's guardian, himself a magi of great skill, watched the shaman prepare his formulations and listened to his incantations. From the spells that he cast, Majeed surmised the shaman had poisoned the prince. The shaman pressed a cloth soaked in his potions first to the lips of ParvAneh and then to the prince and muttered counter-curses while Majeed pulled his dagger from inside his cloak and prepared to drive it into the shaman's neck.

ParvAneh and the prince sighed in one breath while sweat poured from their faces and soaked their clothes. Their forms wavered in the dim light of oil lamps arrayed about the dining hall and in one final shriek of pain they transmuted into forms that the shaman had initially considered an elegant curse to place upon the prince – they were transmuted into a pair of silken haired coursing hounds. When Majeed saw what had been done, he drew the dagger deep across Behrouz's throat. There was no spell that could undo the transmutation of ParvAneh and the prince.

The bus swayed her from side to side, bouncing over lumps and patches in the street. The motion made her stomach float. Before she vomited, Melissa closed her notebook and slid it back into her daypack. She leaned her head back, kept her eyes focused on the ads plastered above the windows, and took deep breaths through her mouth. That's what her mother told her to do when she was little and got carsick. She tried not to taste the air in the bus. The bus was crowded and three blocks down the street she pulled the bell cable and got off. It was a nice afternoon. She would walk for a while and settle her stomach with cool air.

She hoped Basil wasn't watching. She didn't want to look crazy.

Basil made her think of John Cleese. That wasn't right. Cleese was too funny. Robert Mitchum in a Marlow movie was better. Not that Jeffry didn't have a sense of humor, but he had a feeling of weight about him, a seriousness she had thought was extreme.

Mitchum was a good name for him. She smiled and watched the faces of houses that she passed. Robert Mitchum, her father didn't like him. When she grew up he wouldn't let them watch his movies, said he was a, but she couldn't remember exactly what her father said anymore. It didn't matter. She loved the fall in San Francisco.

- Cocobolo -

Disk2

One Halloween when I was 9 or 10, Wallace Jenkins and Bobby Roberts came over to the house. We made the rounds, collecting candy and acting like fools. I had a skeleton costume that glowed in the dark after standing under a light. We had a lot of fun with that, scaring girls when they walked by the old tree out front. We didn't think much about it.

Wallace Jenkins was dressed like a hobo, which was a cheap costume since all his mom had to do was rip up some of his dad's old clothes and rub charcoal on his face. He didn't scare anybody. Bobby Roberts was a baseball player. Big deal. He just wore his little league uniform and his momma got him a Dodgers cap from the store.

We were sitting in the living room eating candy and watching TV when Grandpa Goings came in right in the middle of the Peanuts cartoon. The old man lived in the back room. My dad added it on the back of the house for him after Grandma G died. We were talking about ghosts and he stood in the doorway, kind of spooky like, and listened for a little bit. After a few minutes of that, he walked in and sat down in my dad's chair.

He said, "You boys want to hear a real ghost story?"

We looked at each other. There wasn't anything we could say to stop him so we said, "Yes sir." Back then we always said sir and ma'm. And the old man started in. "You ever hear the story about Ricky Primes?"

"No, sir."

"Ricky's family lived up the road not far from where our place was." The old man pulled out his pipe and pushed some fresh tobacco in it. "Left here for the Navy as soon as he was old enough. Wanted to see the world. Was in for twenty years. Only came home a couple of times in all those years. Came out of the Navy a Chief Petty Officer. Had stripes on his sleeve from his elbow down to his cuff."

The old man held his arm out and showed where Ricky Primes' stripes were. We looked at his arm and watched him draw them with the stem of his pipe. "Ricky was something to see in his uniform. Had ribbons and medals all over his chest."

The old man stopped and lit his pipe, puffing and pulling air until the tobacco glowed red and pipe smoke made a low cloud hanging in the living room. Momma hated the smoke in her house but wouldn't say anything since it was the old man that made it.

"Everybody was surprised when he moved back to his home place. By then his folks had been dead for some time. Nobody was living out there in the house."

The old man stopped talking a minute and smoked his pipe, eyes closed and face relaxed. He seemed to have forgot we were there.

"What about the ghost?" The waiting was killing us.

He opened his eyes and looked at us. "First day back, Ricky pulled up to the store in an old Ford truck. He had somebody, looked like a blond haired woman sitting in the truck with him. Only when we looked close it wasn't a woman. It was a big dog. Long hair, ears blended right into its neck so you couldn't tell they were ears. And it was sitting in his truck on the front seat just like any human being."

We snickered, shoved on each other and said, "or a woman that looked like a dog."

The old man snorted at us, "You kids," and started pushing himself up out of his chair but we were saying no no no we want to hear about the ghost and after a bit of that he sat back down. He said ok but we had to be quiet or he wasn't going to tell it. We said we would be quite and he started up again.

"I went up to him and I asked him, 'Ricky, what kind of dog is that?' Anybody else and we'd have laughed him out of St. Helena but his daddy always had fine dogs so I figured it must be something special.

He said, "It's what's called an Afghan Hound. The Kings of Persia have hunted with them since the age of the Pharaohs."

"We all stood around the front of his truck looking in at that dog while she sat there like the Queen of Sheba looking down at us like we were monkeys in a zoo. Lord that just gave me the creeps. Never had a animal make me feel that way before."

The old man stopped talking a minute and smoked his pipe. We knew all about the Queen of Sheba from Sunday School. On the wall in our Sunday School room was a picture of her meeting King Solomon and she was wearing these thin gauzy robes. I think that's about the only thing any of us ever remembered from church.

"I went over to his house the next day to say hello and get a better look at that dog. When I pulled up in that yard all his coonhounds come out swirling around my truck." The old man made big swirling motions with his arms, pipe griped in his hand, stem pointing out between his clenched fingers like a single black talon. It made him look crazy, like Ahab. We all snickered cause he made us nervous. "I could hardly get my door open for the damn dogs. The whole time I was getting out of the truck I was looking for a glimpse of that Afghan dog.

"I didn't see it anywhere. Since it was a special kind of dog, I figured he might have had it out back. So I went up to the front door and just as I was getting ready to knock I saw her sitting on the sofa looking at me through the window glass. Her front feet were dangling over the edge of the sofa and she looked at me for about a second before she let loose the biggest bark I ever heard. Almost jumped off the front porch. Ricky's wife Wanda came running to the door and invited me in. So I went in and sat in that living room with Wanda and the dog. The dog was sitting on the sofa while me and Wanda was sitting in chairs. Never sat in a living room with a dog sitting on a sofa before. I told Wanda I'd never seen anybody letting a dog get on the furniture and she laughed a little bit and said that Ricky was spoiling it. Said he'd just lost his mind over these dogs when he was stationed out in California. His big plan was to set himself up a kennel and raise them out there at East Fork. I asked her what could you do with a dog like that. It was a good-looking dog and all but it was covered with long hair, worse than any setter you could imagine. No way you could go hunting with it.

"About that time, Ricky walked in and we said hello and he said, 'Come on out back with me, Edgar. I want to show you something.' Then he turned to the dog as we was walking out and he said 'Let's go, Baby.' That was what he called her, Baby. And she just stepped down off that sofa and walked with us out to the back, stepping real dainty down the steps. Didn't look like no hunting dog to me. I wasn't expecting to see much out of it.

"Ricky said, 'Watch this, Edgar.' And he threw a tennis ball out in the field behind his house. Baby took off. I never seen a dog run like that. She was so fast she hardly touched the ground."

The old man stopped again and picked up his pipe, crushing the burned tobacco.

"It was just beautiful. She ran that ball down, whacked it with her front foot as she went by, circled around, picked it off the ground on a dead run with her teeth, flipped it in the air, and caught it. She was a beautiful killing animal. I never seen a dog do that."

The old man stopped talking again and rubbed his old hands on his legs while he smoked his pipe.

"Grandpa, what about the ghost story? Where does that come in?"

He looked down at me. "I'm getting to it.

"Ricky was keeping his dog close to the house. Not letting her out of the backyard or the house. Course he fenced in damn near an acre out back so she could run. Mostly though Baby stayed in the house.

"A few weeks later Myrtle Rogers, his sister-in-law, came over to visit and she let Baby loose out the front door.

"Myrtle didn't approve of them having a dog in the house so she didn't work very hard at stopping Baby from getting out. To Myrtle, a dog was just a animal that lived under the house. I always thought she done it on purpose. She was a ignorant woman, set in her ways.

"Big running dog like Baby, she just took off and next thing you know she got hit by a car down on the highway. She died right there."

The old man stopped talking and just smoked his pipe for a few minutes. All we could see was the Queen of Sheba lying crumpled on the road.

"Mr. G," Bobby Roberts asked, "Wasn't there nothing anybody could do for her?"

The old man put his pipe down. "No, nothing."

Wally said, "That's sad, Mr. G."

The old man said, "It was. Ricky came home from working at the mill and found Baby lying dead on the front porch. Wanda had gone down to the road and got her.

"Once she realized her sister had let Baby out the front door, Wanda went running across the front yard like a crazy woman trying to get that dog back.

"But Baby was too fast. That was one runnin' dog. Nothing but time was going to catch her.

"Wanda made it down to the road, but it was too late. They carried Baby on back up to the house and Wanda laid her out on the porch. It was the only thing she knew to do.

In the meantime, her sister, Myrtle, she took off. She knew better'n be around when Ricky came home and saw Baby laid out there dead."

"What'd Ricky do Grandpa?"

"He walked up on the porch and just collapsed. Sank right down to his knees and cried. Sometimes when you hear stories they say so-and-so cried like a baby. This wasn't no crying like a baby. This here was earth opened up and hell coming out crying. God I never heard such a mournful low wail that just went on an on till there was no air left in his lungs and he dropped over. Made the goose bumps crawl up my arms. That night went by and Ricky, he just sat outside on the porch by his dog. The other dogs they stayed away, they knew something bad had happened. Next morning Ricky got up and dug a hole for Baby out in the yard behind the house. Planted a live oak acorn at the top of her grave."

"Is she the ghost?" Bobby was sitting with his knees pulled up into his chest trying not to cry.

"Well, I ain't done with the story. Ricky was in such a state, next day he couldn't eat and then he got a cough he couldn't shake. A couple of nights later Wanda said while she was sleeping he must've got up in the middle of the night and went out on the porch. She found him out there the next morning curled up on the porch like he was asleep. But when she tried to wake him he was already gone. Doc said he must have caught the walkin' pneumonia stayin' out on the porch all night with Baby.

"Ricky just loved that dog." The old man put the pipe back in his mouth and took a few pulls on it, sending smoke out in the air where it coiled around the ceiling light.

"What about the ghost, Grandpa?" I asked.

"Well, sir, one night, a couple of years after all that, I was driving down that road where Baby got hit. Wasn't far from my place. And I thought I saw something moving 'tween the trees up by Ricky's place so I turned off the road and drove on up there.

"Wanda had moved in to town with her sister after Ricky died so the place was empty again. She had started working at the Pritchard's drugstore stocking shelves. Anyway, I thought it might be a hobo or somebody going up to his place. Maybe some kids going up there to break out his windows. So I drove up and stopped the car.

"When I turned the headlights off, that's when I caught sight of her. She was out there running across that field in the moonlight. Twisting and turning and leaping in the air, just like her and Ricky were still playing.

"And then she was gone. She was only there a moment.

"Every night at dusk I would go back out there hoping I could watch her playing in the field. I pretended she ain't dead. Sometimes I could see her. But not often."

The old man's head dropped on his chest and we could see his shoulders jerking up and down. He was crying without making any sounds, which scared the hell out of us. In a minute, he shoved his way out of the chair and went outside.

When my folks left to take my little brother trick-or-treating, they told me to keep an eye on the old man in case he got sick. He had a bad heart. So I told Wallace Jenkins and Bobby Roberts not to eat my candy, I'd be back in minute and headed out the door after the old man. When I got out there, he was sitting under our tree, smoking his pipe, and watching nothing in the street. Everybody was done with trick-or-treat by that time and gone home. So I went over and sat down by him on one of the roots and asked him if he was ok. He said he was. Said he didn't mean to get so worked up about the ghost story. He hadn't told that one in a long time. I figured probably never.

I told him it was ok. It was a good story anyway. I told him, "Bobby Roberts probably won't be able to sleep tonight thinking about that Afghan dog."

He said, "good."

I laughed and the old man laughed with me a little but not very loud.

I opened my mouth to ask who was driving the car that killed Baby but I couldn't do it. Instead, I sat under the tree like a chicken-shit and watched the old man smoke his pipe and rub his eyeballs with the backs of his fists. I didn't want to hear him say it was him. I ended up not asking or saying anything.

I stayed out there with him long as I could stand it. Bobby Roberts was inside with my candy so as soon as I could, I patted the old man on the back, told him it was ok, and left him sitting in the dark. He was out there until after we were done eating candy and my friends had left to go home, and Momma and Daddy were back with my little brother.

I thought I'd ask the old man about it some day later when he wasn't so sad but I never did. The next year he was dead and he never talked about it again to me or anybody else. I should have made him say that night but I let him off. I didn't want anybody finding out it was my grandpa who killed the Queen of Sheba.

Hannah pulled the disk out of her camera and wrote Disk 2, Baby's Story on it before she slipped it into the plastic sleeve.

"Daddy, is that a true story?"

JB crushed the cigarette out against the snakehead tattoo on the back of his hand.

"Why, Hannah? Did you like that one?"

He leaned back into the warm bark of Baby's oak and closed his eyes.

"Sort of. Did you ever find out who killed Baby?"

"No, but it was the old man. Ironic don't you think? Never got over it either. You ready to get back to town? It's going to be dark soon."

"In a minute. I want to get a shot of you sitting under the oak."

Disk2

Hannah loaded another disk in her camera and filmed until dark.

- Cocobolo -

Author's Notes

The contents of *Sex Life for Ghosts* is based on stories my great grandmother told me about my Cherokee great-great grandparents and how they came to live in Louisiana. People forget that there are Indians still living in Louisiana. The characters in the story are fictional, however. The stories in this piece, told by the great-great-grandmother, are stories of the Cherokee people.

The original title of the story titled *Barista* was *Girl With Dragon Tattoo*. It was a story that developed after seeing the photo of one of my wife's relatives who had gotten a large dragon tattoo of which she was quite proud. I was in a phase at the time where I was naming stories in the style used for paintings and used a minimalist descriptive subject title, *Girl With Dragon Tattoo*, I considered the story name unique and quite beautiful. A year or two after writing that piece I discovered a display table in Page and Palette (my favorite local bookstore and the reason I moved to Fairhope) populated with books titled *The Girl With the Dragon Tattoo*. I was devastated – almost ill. It was a long time before I was able to re-title that story. I protest my loss. Still in my mind, I use the original. I have not yet read the novel by Stieg Larsson. Perhaps I should. In Sweden, it's real title is *Men Who Hate Women*. Sigh

When *Disk2* was originally written it was titled *Tape2*. Technology has changed considerably since that time - and still does. My current camera doesn't use a disk for storage but I gave up trying to shift the title to match current technology. Hopefully that isn't a problem for readers who have no memory of cameras that use removable storage media. I submitted this piece to a short story publication one time and the editor was kind enough to reply that the grandfather was stereotypical and while he recognized it as a frame narrative he didn't like the twist in narration at the end. I considered changing that for a time but never did. The entire point of the piece is that it is a story about a story and while it is a form of frame narrative it's really more metafiction so the twist was not really a twist at all. That was really the point of the piece. I decided not to send it out for publication again.

About that time, I became tired of/bored with revising pieces to fit within word count constraints of journals. That was such an artificial reason to do a revision. And I didn't want to write that way. I like complexity and layering which often become lost or compromised when "tightening up" a piece for a small journal. None of my pieces actually fit within the format requirements for journals anyway so I ended that effort as being noncreative and counterproductive to the craft of writing. I've always been uncomfortable with statements I've made in workshops about someone's story actually beginning deeper in the piece. Perhaps I just didn't get the meaning of the piece – instead of cutting perhaps it needed deeper exploration, more layers and complexity. My sincere late apologies to Jane. We undervalue complexity and obscurity for the sake of comfortable concise definitions.

Clifford Wayne received his MFA in writing from the University of San Francisco., He is a member of the Association of Writer's and Writing Programs, the Alabama Writer's Forum, and is currently working on his PhD at the University of South Alabama. Born in Canton, Mississippi, he grew up in La Place, Louisiana, and lived most of his adult life in Texas and California. He now resides in Alabama with his wife Theresa and two Afghan Hounds, Niki and Howl.